Flower Among Ash

Angela James

LifeRich
PUBLISHING

Copyright © 2017 Angela James.

All rights reserved. No part of this book may be used or reproduced by any means, graphic, electronic, or mechanical, including photocopying, recording, taping or by any information storage retrieval system without the written permission of the author except in the case of brief quotations embodied in critical articles and reviews.

LifeRich Publishing is a registered trademark of
The Reader's Digest Association, Inc.

LifeRich Publishing books may be ordered
through booksellers or by contacting:

LifeRich Publishing
1663 Liberty Drive
Bloomington, IN 47403
www.liferichpublishing.com
1 (888) 238-8637

Because of the dynamic nature of the Internet, any web addresses or links contained in this book may have changed since publication and may no longer be valid. The views expressed in this work are solely those of the author and do not necessarily reflect the views of the publisher, and the publisher hereby disclaims any responsibility for them.

Any people depicted in stock imagery provided by Thinkstock are models, and such images are being used for illustrative purposes only.
Certain stock imagery © Thinkstock.

ISBN: 978-1-4897-1334-6 (sc)
ISBN: 978-1-4897-1333-9 (e)

Library of Congress Control Number: 2017910917

Print information available on the last page.

LifeRich Publishing rev. date: 07/18/2017

Contents

Seeing the Omega 2
When the Dust Settled 12
Shooting the Breeze 18
It's a Dirty Job 26
Foot-Mouth Disease 36
Misconception 52
Well Oiled Plan 60
What Now! 66
Where are my Books? 70
Movie and a Blankie 82
Carbon Footprint 88
One Caucasian Boy 94
Extended Church 108
Sticking Around 112
Not a Fan 124
Bridging the Gap 136
Hands off Training 146
Staying Connected 152
TAG! You're It 156
Milestone Reached 160
This is Awkward. 166
Out-doing Each Other 172

Here we are Again 180
Kiss and Ride 202
Walking in Integrity 226
Black Blonde 236
What did Paul Say? 242
Sunny Side Up 248
Rewind and Replay 250
She Forgot 254
The Testimony 260

Seeing the Omega

It was the 12th of August 2007 in a dingy one-bedroom apartment in Parkdale in Toronto where Taniqua called home. She and her children had to call this dilapidated building their home because neither Taniqua and the father of her children had a salary. The little they had from the government and food banks in the surrounding community still wasn't enough for a decent livable apartment in Toronto.

The humidity was above the seasonal weather in the city and the days old garbage was evident as the odor penetrate the vicinity and through the creases of the windowsill. The sweltering heat prevented the occupants from opening the window for fresh air. The small dollar store fans were place different places in the room to replace what was the AC.

To make matters worse, the walls were peeling and falling onto the floor. You would think that the ministry of housing would've condemn this apartment but where would they go?

Duquan emerges from the bedroom. He was on the phone with Ketrel. He was dressed like the stereotypical young man his age in that part of the community. At least more than 75% of men his age wore their pants exposing their boxers with just a undershirt that was tucked into his boxers.

His hair was neatly braided, and neck, ears, fingers, and mouth was filled with jewelry. He is a well-groomed metrosexual young man who is meticulous about his grooming and appearance but when it comes to spending his money in the home or for his family; he neglects that responsibility.

Duquan is a very handsome guy and very charming but

he lacks moral and accountability where it counts. At least that is how Taniqua feel most of the time.

"Where you at man? Say what, man! You know you were supposed to pick me up like yesterday. Are you for real? The ride stalled. You're playing me. Are you for real?. Put the car in neutral and push it bro. I just got to get there like now. Say what! You never come through for me dog. Yes! Dog! It's no big deal man, take all the time in the world".

After realizing that Ketrel was running late he slumped into the sofa feeling let down. The pointed edges of a toy caused him to leap out of the sofa faster than a bolt of lightning. He quickly and angrily rummage through the unfolded laundry on the sofa to uncover what caused the discomfort. It was a happy meal toy. He took it out from among the laundry and tossed across the room infuriatedly.

"Hey Taniqua, how many times must I tell you not to leave your little maggots toys on the furniture. The toy almost ran up my derriere. Don't you think it is time for you to get up out of the bed and clean up around here" He looked around the apartment in disgust," Poverty is a crime, I need to leave this dump at any cost".

Taniqua came out of the bedroom dressed in a skimpy summer that revealed her pregnancy. She put her extension up in a ponytail that hangs down her back with a bang in the front that accentuate her slender face. She like Duquan was wearing a few jewelries though not as much.

"Look Duquan, I am sick and tired of you calling my children maggots. And FYI, they are yours too! Why can't you clean up this place? I waddle to the laundry mat, did the laundry plus folding them: you could at least put them away before the kids unfolded them.", she argued with him.

"That's your job", he replied under his breath.

"Pardon me? What was that?

"Why do you have to be hostile all the time?

"Isn't it obvious".

"You're losing it. Nothing coming out of your mouth make any sense".

"For once you got it right. I was losing it when I went down town to bail you out two days ago. I was losing it when I allowed you to knocked me up again".

Dequan interrupted her, "Wait a minute! I did not hear you complaining. As a matter of fact you're the one always begging me to stay with you", he continued feeling like a peacock to be needed to the point of her pending all that she had just to be with him.

"I should have left you locked up" she answered.

"Whatever"

"Whatever! You are ungrateful, you know that. Look at my living room. It is a pig's sty since you've been here. This apartment was never like this and you got the nerve hollering out my name to come a clean up after you. I bet if I had a lighter and brighter complexion, I wouldn't have this problem", she replied in disgust of him.

Duquan redial trying to get Ketrel. He got his voice mail. "It is always something with you", he told Taniqua and locked himself in the bathroom.

She banged on the door. "I know that you are not using the phone. You cannot get away from me. We need to talk Duquan! I've had enough! She screamed through the door. She continued to speak with a sense of hopelessness, "I am sick and tired of you using me to bail you out when things are tight with you and your so-called friends turn their backs on you. This is the last time Duquan. I guess my black isn't that beautiful for you anymore. This tar baby is through with you. As a matter of fact, when you are through please leave so that me and my maggots can live our lives in peace".

"It is not like I am not trying to change", he replied as he reentered the living room.

"You are not trying hard enough. I'm always the backup plan when everything else fails. Now what. Are you going to leave me again to support our children all by myself?

"You just told me to leave"

"So"

"That is why…

"Why what Duquan? Am I too charcoal for you?"

"Ghetto more like it"

"I live in the ghetto, dah! Therefore, I am ghetto"

"You don't have to act like it"

Taniqua spirit became more somber. She spoke with hopelessness in her voice. You could hear the tragedy in each word. They were becoming more meaningful as she confesses them. She was sore disappointed in her choices that held her in captivity. She wondered how she could be this blind and naive.

She spoke carefully," This is my reality Duquan and you are responsible for whom I am and moreover it is men like you that causes women like me to act ghetto because people like you take us for their door mats and your 7/11. What am I supposed to do? I had dreams until you told me all those lies Duquan. I left my mama's house without responsibilities and traded it is for this dump".

The words were leaving her mouth as she tried to make

sense of her speech. She continues listlessly, "Why don't you clean up your act? Ingrid told me she saw you at the Laundromat washing one of your plastic girlfriend's clothes and she left you there to dry and fold all by yourself. Why can't you do that for own flesh and blood?

"I do not know what you're talking about"

"Selective amnesia eh?

"Ingrid is a liar. She wants to break us up. Tell her to stop watching me"

"Get a clue then you can converse with me"

"Look who is talking"

Her extensions seemed to be tearing up either from the humidity or her sad story. The tracks of her tears stained her face as she braced the doorpost and sigh with regret.

"I never thought I would come to this. It was all about you and being a family. Look at me! Barefooted and pregnant, living off welfare, shopping at thrift stores and food banks. How did I fall in love with you? If I had only listen to mama. There is no hope for me Duquan but you can be a man and don't let this happen to our girls. I swear, after this one, I am tying my tube, better yet, I am having a hysterectomy. I hope it is not too late for me. I am in pain and look at you just sitting there as if I do not exist. Is it so hard for you to hug me like you used to, kiss me like that first magical kiss in the movie theatre? What did I do that was so wrong to make you change from me? I never cheated on you, I'm always here for you, bailing you out and having your babies. Go. Do not wait for an excuse, I know what I have to do now".

She was too tired to speak or gave up because it seems

as if she was not getting through to him. She disappeared into the room and Duquan hit the redial again.

"Dog where are you? She going off again, I need a ride dog. Say what! TTC" lowering his voice and watching the bedroom door if Taniqua heard him. "I am not going out like this, I do not ride the bus. I'm not Rosa Parks. The agency is still open; are you helping me or what? Cool, see you in five" He spoke to himself with dismay. "This is not how I'd seen my life Taniqua but the POPO changed all that. Sorry babe but you know how it goes, there is no bligh for the black man in Toronto. I have to make my own way; the only way I know"

His thoughts were broken by the screams coming from the bedroom. He ran into the room to see what had happened.

"My water broke, call 911!"

"Are you sure?

"Yes I am s-u-r-e, the baby is coming. Don't just stand there, we've done this two times before. Move it! We are finished!"

He hit redial for the third time, Ketrel, she is having the baby, yes, where are you?

"Duquan, are you on the phone with Ketrel at a time like this? I told you to call 911".

"And I heard you but he is in the lobby and the ambulance will take forever to get here. You remember when the pizza delivery guy couldn't find the apartment and if he is a delivery guy and he could not find it, how is the ambulance supposed to find us and don't tell me he did that to scam us out of a free pizza".

"Oh gosh! Now is not the time to go mad".

There was a rapid knock at the door.

"Ketrel is here". He went and answered the door. "You stink man".

"That is the smell of a hardworking man, where she at?

Taniqua was already at the bedroom door with her packed bag. "Let's go".

Ketrel did not move. Taniqua and Duquan looked at him in amazement.

"You know my license was suspended and I cannot drive because of the heat. It's stalled. It's the starter, I think" Ketrel tried to piece his sentences together.

"I am surrounded by stooges! I've surrounded myself with fools and losers that serve me right", she muttered to herself. She was leading them out of the apartment. The guys followed after her.

"I told you to go to one of them Starbuck and wait till the baby comes, at least my son would be on the six o'clock news; you know what I'm saying."

"You are an idiot! Did you call the ambulance!?"

"No. The phone got cut off"

"Where is the stupid elevator when you need it?"

"Dog, I thought you hang up on me. Your phone got cut off like that? It's tight with you"

"I am going to die with these two black stooges", she screamed with the intense pain and contractions.

"If I am a stooge then why are you waiting for a broken elevator. Yeah! who is the stooge now? Duquan said trying to level the playing field."

"You are both stooges for letting me wait, and the baby is coming. I'm not going to make it, Call the ambulance from your cell Ketrel".

"I only have three minutes left and they will put you on hold", he said foolishly.

"Stop! I don't want to hear it! Move out of my way and let my try this door", she said and pushed them out of her way to get to the door.

She knocked on the neighbor's door rapidly with her fist. Luckily someone was home to help her. The ambulance did come but her son had already entered the world; three doors down from her apartment. She named him DJ shortened for Duquan Junior. She pondered if it was a good choice to name him after his father but this was his son and she still loves him.

When the Dust Settled

Ketrel dropped by the apartment the following Sunday after DJ was born. Duquan was still asleep after a heavy late lunch. Taniqua let him in the apartment to keep him from waking up the colicky baby. She was first furious with him when DJ's sleep was disturbed from her trying to communicate with him that she was on her way to open the door and the baby was asleep. Luckily for him, DJ fell back to sleep with a few gently pat on the back.

"What do you want Ketrel?"

"Where's Duquan?

"Your dog is in his kennel as usual. I would like to know what you have on him why he jumps to your every request and seems to be as deaf as a log when I ask him to do anything for his own children. I need your training secret", she told him jokingly.

"We've been together since daycare"

"Sounds like a marriage. So, what's going down today?"

"Nothing".

"Really! If you get him in any trouble, I will not be that person going to the police station and to bail him out again. He is your dog but when the rubber meets the road, you all bail on him like everybody else".

"It's not like that" Duquan is his own problem. I am a hard worker. I have mouths to feed and I am not about to be like my old man you know and walk away from my responsibilities because of a woman. I got no GED but I make do with what I can get. By the way, he is coming with me today"

"To do what?"

"Work."

"Duquan work! I must see this with my own two eyes. He is afraid of work like the devil is afraid of holy water. What type of work? Sorry for the mess. Move the laundry over and have a seat. They are clean. Let me go and get him for you".

Taniqua went into the bedroom to get Duquan up, "Hey get up. Ketrel is in the living room. He said that he is here to pick you up for work. How comes you didn't tell me that you got a job", she probes him.

Duquan ignore her questioning by engaging the twins in horse play. He came out of the bedroom with the twins hanging on to his legs for the ride. He scratched and yawned like an uncivilized person.

"What did I ever saw in you, you disgust me", Taniqua said in disgust.

"You know you love a good rugged man, right Ketrel".

"The cornmeal porridge ready yet mommy?" Tanisha asked squeezing her way through the little space in the almost blocked doorway by her father.

"I would like some of that too hun", Duquan said teasing Taniqua.

Ignoring her daughter's question; she continued to address Duquan. "A man doesn't work; he does not eat; so, the good book says. You already had your portion. The left over is for Rae and Raven. She took the twins into the bathroom for a quick shower before they eat. She called out from the bathroom, "please do not eat the kids' food Duquan! It's about time you get a job. I do not understand your thinking. You have no skills and yet you're waiting for that perfect job that you are not qualify for. I will not tolerate you fermenting on my Goodwill sofa any longer. I am giving you one more week or else. You better make it work this time and no more excuses".

"Or else what? Duquan asked acting manly.

Flower Among Ash

That was not a good question for Duquan to ask Taniqua a week after she had giving birth to his son. It was as if she was possessed. She pulled the twins by their scrawny arms out of the bathroom dripping from their bath. "What did you say?! I told you this was it and I'm not going to have you sit up in here till things start going your way for you to walk out on me again. It is going to be different this time. You know what?" She paused, "I am going to Gorge Brown College to get a degree and dump your sorry, sick good for nothing self. You disgust me".

"College. Don't crack me up. College! You're too old for college and more over you are not college material. You are not leaving the ghetto. Here you live and here you shall be buried with all of us. We are all going to die here. This is it baby; our past, present and future. Get your head out of the clouds tar baby! We are not cut out for nothing more than this. College? Must be Clown College"

She rushed in and out of the room like a whirlwind to get towels to wrap the twins in and hurriedly gave them their meal. "Yes Duquan, I know that I am a tar baby for you but my black is beautiful for someone else. Stop blocking my blessing", she responded angrily. "I hope Lydia makes you happy being fair skin and all".

"Lydia who?"

"You know we are the same age in the same situation and both African descent. The only difference is that her complexion is just a bit lighter than mine. Are you going to support her and her children too? And by-the-way, she recently went back to school".

"Are you competing?

"I thought you didn't know who I was talking about".

Ketrel interjected, "sorry to break up all this love talk but we have to go".

"She graduated from high school. She also did two years at the University of Toronto. What do you have?"

"All this about a woman you do not know".

"Ok. Break it up. Taniqua, go for it girl. One of us should at least go for a piece of the pie. I try to get Ingrid to do something with herself and told her I will take care of things but she is all about party and welfare. Welfare is what they give us to feel relax and complacent, to keep us trap"

"Say what? Mind them big words give you nose bleed" Duquan snubbed him.

"I almost got my high school degree and that is why I am still having a hard time finding a decent job. I wish you all the best and talk to Ingrid, maybe you can influence her in doing something with herself", Ketrel applauded her.

Outrageously, Duquan lashed out on him, "how dare you come up in my crib encouraging my woman to leave me dog? Get stepping. Leave! I thought you were my dog"

"Nobody is talking about anybody breaking up. Why you must be that way? I want the best for you dog, and her. She is like my sister, dog. Get your act together and support the sista. Why would you think I would do something like that? You know me better than that. Remember, I was the one that got you guys back together for the kids' sake, make it work this time"

Detouring from the subject he took the twins and went into the bedroom to get them dressed. "Apparently, your mother's head is in the cloud talking about college that she forgot to get you dressed. What a joke".

Ketrel pushed aside the laundry on the sofa and indicate

to Taniqua to sit and tell him more about her idea about going to college. Duquan took the twins into the bathroom to brush the twins' teeth while eavesdropping on the discussion between Ketrel and Taniqua. Finally, he joined them in the living room. "You think the government is going to give you money to go to college".

"I can apply for OSAP and by the looks of it, I might be qualified because of my situation"

"How is that suddenly you want to go to school and what situation are you talking about?

She ignored him and continued to talk to Ketrel, "Tomorrow I am going to George Brown to see if they have space and have students' services tell me what I need to do to be accepted and then I will pass the info to you for Ingrid".

"Don't you have to be a student to go to student services for help? You have not gotten accepted yet and you're acting like you are already a student there. That is blind faith"

"Don't you have somewhere you have to go?"

"My gosh! We late dog! Let's roll, and by the way, we taking the bus"

Taniqua looked at him sternly with unspoken words that say he better say all the right words or else something was going to give. He avoided making eye contact with her and headed quickly towards the door.

"I'll be back by dinner time"

"You funny, you so funny. You'll be back by dinner. You'll be back by dinner when you bring home dinner"

Taniqua sat in disbelief of the wheels in motion she started. She questioned herself, "is it possible for her to go back to school? Was Duquan right? Her pride was now propelling her forward. She has no other choice but to move forward with her plan.

Shooting the Breeze

Flower Among Ash

Ingrid and Taniqua's children had a play-date in the parkette at the front of the apartment building. They sat on the bench facing the sandbox catching up on the events of their lives. The girls talked about anything that came to mind. They became people watchers as other parents joined them at the parkette park which fuel their conversation.

Taniqua had her eyes fastened on a blond Caucasian girl playing in the sandbox next to Tanisha. She nudged Ingrid with her elbow to get her attention to what was going on. "Did you see that? She just walked over to Tanisha and picked up the pail. I cannot believe it! And Tanisha just sit there and let her".

"I do not think Tanisha was using it", Ingrid replied.

"That is not the case; it is just the way she did it".

"Tanisha seems to be ok about it"

"No! It is the act of walking over and taking something that is sitting right before someone else"

"I guess she is the type of person to take what she wants. I'm just kidding", Ingrid said jokingly. "You're not racist, are you?

"What kind of question is that? How can I be racist? She is privileged.", Taniqua insisted.

"You are not making any sense to me right now. And by the way, Racism is in every culture and race including us. We are not immune".

"Call me prejudice but not racist", Taniqua explained.

Don't let it bother you. If Tanisha was using it, then, we would have to fix that and you know I would!"

"That sounds so ghetto", Taniqua informed Ingrid.

"Look at you now, calling me ghetto", Ingrid replied in a snobbish way. "You're the one to call people ghetto. We're are both sailing in the same ship. As Michael Jackson says, look at the man in the mirror".

"Ok, my apology. It is more than that. I have always wondered what make a girl like that goes around with such confidence. She saw the pale and she did not think twice to take it. Do you think it is lack of self-confidence, assertiveness, or knowledge why we act so defeated before we try anything? I wonder if Tanisha would have asked her for the pale instead of taking it?

"Black children are taught manners. We had to be respectful or feast on some knuckle sandwich or a few stripes to correct our waywardness and we are not even Christians. Where would they learn that? Unless their parents told them to act that way"

"Or maybe, their parents who got the good jobs and are able to give their children whatever they need so they do not know what it is like to lack anything. They are used to getting whatever they want so they take things".

"Or, they could be spoiled" Ingrid suggested.

"Some black children are spoiled" Taniqua thought to herself.

"One of my biggest *pet peeve* is seeing black child in the Shopping Mall having a tantrum for something silly and to make it worst, the parents that cease to parent their children"

"It is from growing up in Jamaican. We could never do that to our parents. I got away with a lot since I got to Canada and look how I turned out", Taniqua said discouragingly. "I am not saying I am the model parent but sometimes I see myself doing the same thing my mom did to me when I was growing up in Jamaica", she continued.

"That is the answer to your question; children act in sandboxes based on how they are raised"

"I still think there is more behind that; I think it is an innate thing they acquire from birth. It could be automatic"

"Do you ever think that as a black person, the way we act around our children and what we say make them act the way they do. It is like, if we keep talking like this in front of our children saying how black people have it hard and life sucks, then they live their lives based on what they hear".

"Are you saying that it is our fault. By backing down or believing that we are underprivileged, we are passing that belief from one generation to another".

"Taniqua! You're unto something. Caucasian people do not have the power over us, we just think that way and then we project that to our children. You got it!"

"I got it at first, then I lost it", Taniqua replied feeling confused.

"What are you not getting? Black people do have some privilege. Like my cousin told me some time ago when she was applying for Teachers College at York University. They have a program where when she indicated on the application that she is Black, they would have considered her application for entrance more favourable. I cannot remember what it was called. It's at the tip of my tongue; what was it? Anyhow, she did not get in"

"How was that a privilege?

"It is like taking all the applicants that are black and review their application more favourable, so more minority can get into the program"

"But she did not get into the program"

"Her grade was poor"

"Really! Or is it that they took all the minority applications and shred them"

"She showed me her grades. It was embarrassing. I stick to what I do best; taking care of my children and I am giving myself all A's",

"You talked about looking in the mirror earlier. Do you have a mirror? You look a mess and your kinky roots are showing. What is it with you? Fix yourself up before you leave the apartment and put on some jewellery, make-up or something", Ingrid told her scornfully. "Stop worrying about things you have no control over. We are who we are".

"Jewellery is not important to me these days. I have my mind on other things".

"Like going back to school. Ketrel told me"

"That was just me thinking out loud and he seams interested"

"Stop fooling yourself Taniqua, we missed our chances. School is not for us. I agree with Duquan. Take your head out of the clouds and accept life as it is and that is why you are becoming so critical about the little white girl who have done nothing to you".

She continues to speak without replying to Ingrid's comment about her wanting to go to school. "If I could read her thoughts"

"I can you assure neither her or her mama are not thinking about getting a welfare cheque or getting food at the food bank at the end of the month" Ingrid assured her.

"And how do you know all this my wise comrade?

"Number one, the way she dresses, and the Mercedes that dropped her off. I bet it was her husband that let her off and then take off to work. Did you not see how distinguish he looked in his pinned stripped suit? She is just here because it is the closest park to her work. People like that don't live here".

Taniqua interrupted Ingrid, "You should be a detective because I saw none those things. The criminal justice needs people like you", she said laughing remembering the advertisement on TV. "But seriously, do you think we will ever get out of this rut?

"What rut? As the Bible say, the poor you will always have among you"

"But does it have to be us?

"You need to stop beating up on yourself. Our parents have nothing so where would we get stuff, besides Jesus said not to lay up treasure here on earth"

"Do you think God pre-destine those whom will forever be poor?

"God gives the freedom of choice to everyone of us"

"So we choose to be poor? I do not think so! Taniqua answered angrily.

"That is not what I am getting at. We should be content in whatever state we are at"

"So what does that makes me?

"A dreamer who simply wants more"

"Is that so wrong?

"If it is going to consume you like this, its not meant to be"

"I know what the Bible say and I try to…. And then again…I am an unwed parent. I guess I dug the pit I am in now"

"Taniqua, we are from poor families from a Third World country. We started with nothing, no inheritance or trust fund"

"And I did not make it any better when I got pregnant just before graduating from high school"

"Let it go! You are human and humans make mistakes. You're entitled to make mistakes here and there"

"One that changed my future"

"OK! You are getting me down. Change the subject please"

"I guess I was born to be a poor person with a humongous dream"

"What are you going to do when your dreams don't come true?

"I do not know. I think my dreams give me hope to reach the light at the end of the tunnel"

"The light at the end of the tunnel could be a freight train. It is a big risk to have dreams and that is why I live in the moment, day by day. The Bible says I should be content and give thanks with what the Lord blessed me with and that is what I planned to do. This is my destiny. You on the other hand need to get use to this"

"How can I? I've always have big dreams. I remembered waiting anxiously for my mother to come for us and how when I get here I was going to be a big star. I've been in Canada for more than a decade now and I am no closer to my dream than when I was living in Jamaica", Taniqua said sadly.

"This goes back to destiny. This is your calling"

"To be a single parent?!

"Do not bite my head off! Changing the subject. God is in control and if He does nothing about your situation, then it means you are living your life accordingly"

"It is free choice…. sometimes. Last night I was

watching the Ten Commandments, you remember the part when the master builder wanted that girl from the mud pit and she was refusing to go. Why is it that things like this don't happen to me?

"It goes to show you Taniqua, you can take a pig out of the mud but you can't take that desire to go roll into the mud out of the pig. If it is in you to do something, then that is your calling, or something like that"

"It was her calling to get out of the mud pit and she wanted to stay with her people, how noble".

"You see; she was content with being a slave. People should accept whatever state they are in. Everyone is not cut out to be rich and famous and besides, it is just a movie"

"That happens in life" Taniqua confirmed.

"Is it raining? City Pulse did not say it was going to rain. Lets go inside and stop all this nonsense"

"The weather channel said it would be just a few sprinkles. It might stop"

"I am getting the kids", Ingrid said and ran off with her children.

"A little raindrop won't kill them. I use to love walking in the rain when I was in Jamaica"

"Well, this is not Jamaica and I will see you later"

"I'll catch up with you later"

Ingrid wanted to get away from Taniqua, "I won't be home. I am going out"

"Where?

"Ketrel is surprising me", she said and disappeared into the building.

It's a Dirty Job

Flower Among Ash

Duquan was sitting in the hallway watching Ketrel pulling the cleaning supplies towards him.

"It feels like a furnace inside here, couldn't they have left the air-conditioner on since they knew we would be here. Man, we can't catch a break", Duquan complained.

"Why don't you stop your whining and come and help me haul the stuff. You should earn your keeps bro. Let's go, we are already running late. Let's go bro!".

Duquan ran to catch up with Ketrel, "So you never told me what the actual job is".

He pointed inside the women's washroom stall, "That"

He walked passed Ketrel looking like the cat that ate the canary, "I always wondered what it would be like to be in the girls' washroom".

Ketrel opened on of the stall."Welcome! now get scrubbing"

"What?"

He pushed opened another stall, "there, that is how we are going to get pay".

"You are out of your cotton-picking mind if you think I am going to clean up anybody's poop"

"Seriously!"

"Why you tripping K?

"It's a dirty job but we got to do it", Ketrel replied.

"Not me bro. I'm outta here".

"One word. Taniqua. NO! Your four children. Their poop is just like ours".

"No way their stool, poop, whatever! Is like mine".

"What color is your stool?"

"Black"

"Really"

"I said it is black"

"Is there something you want to tell me bro. Are you dying on me?

"I'm cool. The iron tablets I got for this anemia thingy"

"For a minute there I thought you be tripping on something, but before that it was brown. Following me. On the other hand, you should see a doctor or something. That's is just creepy".

"Sure".

"Look at that! same color as yours before the so-called iron tablets and you my friends get the opportunity to unclog this one. Your dream has now come true, to be in a woman's washroom. There is the plunger, help yourself. Think of the hard cash you will be taking home to your woman and the nice delectable dinner you and your family will be having tonight. Look ahead bro, not at what is before you"

"How could I not see what is before me?"

It was dead silence for a while except for the scrubbing until toilet water splashed on Duquan's Timberland, "Crap! crap! CRAP!"

Ketrel called out from the opposite stall, "Call it what you want bro if when you are finish, you can either see your face in the bowl or eat off it"

"I'm out of here. My boots man! I paid $120 for this"

"And you cannot feed your family? Money that could've feed your family?

"I am not going to do this anymore"

Ketrel was at the end of his rope. "Suit yourself. When are you going to be a man? I got you a job at UPS and you complained that you cannot get up so early in the morning. I hook you up with this gig and you are going to roll out on me. What about me? How must I finish this job all by myself before the boss gets here? Think about someone other than yourself D. I've seen you worked harder when you were whupped by your vanilla ice whom you could not touch half of the time but pose up like things was all that, your trophy girls. It's ok. I got this", Ketrel told him disappointedly.

Sulking, "I rather go back to UPS"

"That ship has sailed big baby".

"You mean this is it?"

"It is not that bad. Until something better comes along. It is only temporary. As I said before, don't look at what is before you, keep your eyes on the bigger prize. It is an honest living and I'm not ashamed of what I do".

"A decent living smelling like human waste. Tell me how did I get to this point"

"Dropping out of school and dealing drugs. The grass is not always greener on the other side".

"It isn't greener at this side either"

Laughing at himself, he replied, "It is depressing but someone has to do it and unfortunately, that is us, for now. You know, I cannot get Taniqua out of my mind".

Duquan stormed out of the stall he was cleaning and pushed the door of the stall open where Ketrel was in violently that the purse holder wedge into the wall of the stall, "Come again, you be thinking about my woman"

For a few seconds Ketrel was speechless, "I don't roll that way man. Chill"

"I don't want you to be thinking about my woman"

Ketrel sat on the toilet, "I understand why you don't want to do this type of jobs and I don't want to continue to do this and when she said she wants to go to college, it made me start thinking. That could be the only way out of this. We should get serious about a better future. This should be temporary. I tried once but when I thought about the years I would have to spend in school, I just walked away"

"I never like school. Mrs. Zimmerman always picked on me. Nothing I did was ever good enough to get a good grade".

"I hear you. She was tough".

"She was a racist. I was tired of falling. If I was going to spend all that time in school and fail may as well I drop out. At least when I am out here, I am not picked on or ridiculed all the time".

"You would think the community would be the jungle but school was a nightmare".

"It was all about surviving, even now, everything is about surviving. How much am I going to get for cleaning all this crap"

"Sixty big ones. Don't spent it all in one place".

"No Frills. Let me see. I have to take home something for dinner"

"Mac and cheese is three for a dollar, dollar daze is still going on".

"I can get a lot of frozen juice, apple juice for DJ"

"Don't forget diaper and wipes"

"She uses wet rag. She is big on saving every penny she can for them kids. I feel like eating a big slice of pizza and a long glass of lemonade"

"You earned it"

"You have something line up for tomorrow?"

"Wow! When you have your head in the toilet for hours,

things started looking more realistic to you, eh? Putting things into perspective?

"Well, let's do this and get out of here".

"No dispute here"

Bringing Home the Bacon

Duquan was thrilled that he could purchase grocery for his family. He has been trying to get on Taniqua's good side since DJ was born, hoping to move from the sofa back to the bedroom. His anticipation of seeing the look on her face and the children sitting around him eating pizza and macaroni and cheese made him feel accomplished. The apartment was in total darkness except for the streetlight coming through the bare window. He stumbled over a few toys as he headed towards the table.

He yelled for Taniqua. "Baby mama! your man is home. Girl I got some great deal at No Frills" As he took out the grocery from the plastic bags, he announced every item that she could hear him. "I got a bunch of banana for only fifty-nine cents off the clearance rack and I got apples, kiwi. I raided the clearance rack baby. Plus, I got macaroni and cheese and instant noodles. Taniqua, don't you hear me, your man is home"

She dragged herself into the living room, "Keep it down babe, the kids are sleeping."

"Get them up! I brought macaroni and cheese and pizza. Put some water to boil and I'll wake them up. There is so much to eat babe. I bought grocery for us baby. Boil the water"

He went into the bedroom and woke up the children. Duquan picked up the twins and return to the living room with the children barely awake. "Boil the water and make the macaroni and cheese, bring the pizza so I can feed the kids"

Taniqua came and slouched next to him in the half wobble sofa. She spoke half asleep, "It's too late and we can't eat everything in one night. Leave the macaroni and cheese for tomorrow"

Duquan was too overjoyed to respond to her request. He shook the twins awake and fed them the pizza. He turned his attention to Taniqua and began to shake her too, "I got you a pop. Guest what kind I got. Guess. Crush. I know how you like Crush. Have some pizza babe before it gets cold"

"For crying out loud man, you're stuffing their faces while they are sleeping. Are you going to choke them to death?

"Tanisha is feeding herself", he replied.

"In her sleep. Give me my kids. You crazy"

She put the children back to bed. He went in after her with the pizza.

"I don't want to eat alone baby. I got this for you guys"

"Goodnight Duquan"

"But Taniqua. You are one cold woman"

He went to the sofa and sat in disbelief. This was not how he saw it played out in his head. He turned on the television and slumped back into the sofa. He realized the pile of clean folded laundry on the lazy boy. "I guess she is tired" He closed his eyes and was about to drift off to sleep when she came out of the room and said, "I will have two slices and that's it. Where is my Crush"

"I thought you were sleeping"

"You have no idea what I hear in my sleep"

He was delighted to serve her. It reminded him of their first date and how things were between them when they first met. They ate, watched a movie, and fell asleep together in the sofa.

Foot-Mouth Disease

Flower Among Ash

It was a typical evening in Toronto. The summer heat and fumes from vehicles was at it's peek and still the squeegee kids could hustle. The humidity blanketed the city under its shade. People shopping and teens hanging out at the mall just to escape the heat. It was almost time for Duquan to go to work. Taniqua had just entered the apartment with some books in her hands. Speaking excitedly about her advancement with school as she walked over to the table to put down her books.

"I got all the info I need to go to college. I went online and applied for OSAP. I had my grades from high school that makes me a shoe-in for college. Good that I was doing AP courses and summer school. I had totally forgotten that I was completing extra credits. Anyways, it would appear that I am qualified for college and if I need additional courses, I still can get in by making up for those electives. Babe, they gave me so much information my head is still spinning".

Duquan spoke to her in a fatherly tone, "You went behind my back and apply for college?! These are the things we must talk about first before you go and do something dumb like that. I wish you would take your head out of the clouds because no way you're going to college. Don't get your hopes up because it is not going to happen!".

"I know you're not talking to me. I have more than enough credit and community service hours through Pathfinder and high school to make me qualify unlike you", she informed him.

"Who is going to take care of the kids when you are at school"

"Their daddy. They do have a daddy?"

"They must have another daddy because you are not

talking about me. I am not babysitting while you run off to college"

"They are your children too. I recall a certain somebody playing in the park and throwing Frisbee with some kid that was not his, voluntarily'

"Why must you always go there?"

"It baffles me as to why you cheat on me with women with kids and you have no problem taking them to the park or the ice-cream parlor with any complaint"

"Well, school is out of the question"

"OK. Wait a bit, did I ask your permission? I don't recall me asking you if I can turn my life around from the big mistake I've made"

"Our relationship is a big mistake?"

"So why won't you marry me?"

It felt like a bulldozer had run over Duquan. He was floored.

"You proposed to Heather and she turned you down"

"This is a competition?"

"I am the mother of your children. The only four, f-o-u-r" she spelled out "that you have unless there are more than I do not know about"

"I turned her down. You get that straight. She wanted *moi*", he informed he feeling full of himself.

"And she dumped *toi*" she replied sounding condescending, "Tell me prince Duquan, what happened?"

Changing the subject, "What's wrong with working at McDonalds?", he asked her.

"I want more with or without you"

"And what then?"

"It depends on if you want to continue to be a jerk. We

have four children in a one-bedroom apartment. If we were white folks, each child would have their own bedroom. I want better and I will work for it. I need your support. You of all people want to be called sugar daddy while most days you cannot buy French Fries for your own kids".

"I am not going to work all night and then to baby sit all day while you go to school to make me look like no chump. I am not going out like that"

Tapping him on his forehead, "Are you in there? Look! I can see that this conversation is over. If you'd love me at all you would support me. If you love your children, you would back me up, but since I am just a fall back relationship, it is evident that I have been fooling myself and you will never marry me and I have to do this on my own"

With a flattering smile on his face, "Are you asking me to marry you?"

"You'd wish. Not after this conversation. It's over, Duquan. You can stay until you get an apartment. There is no future for us. I am not going to waste my wish upon a star for you to come around and love us or support us".

"You are kicking me out? Who is going to take care of the kids?"

"Don't feel sorry for my children, you are hardly in their lives already and besides, OSAP will give me enough until I've completed my studies"

"Sounds like a well-oiled plan but you are…"

"No! I am winging it. All I want is to get into school and move on with my life, without you"

They were interrupted by a knock on the door. Taniqua answered the door. "Hey Ketrel"

He was too excited to see the sadness on her face. He

hugged her and picked her up and spun her around. "You are the greatest"

"Boy put down my woman!" Duquan demanded

"Dog, I got great news. Taniqua brought some info from the college for Ingrid but she told me she was content with her part-time job and thing, basically, school is not for her. It got me thinking…."

"Infiltrator. Another relationship you want to break up", Duquan interrupted him.

"It is not like that. I call for some info, to make a long story short, I called my old high school and they told me I just need a few more credits to complete my high school degree and there is more dog"

"How short is this tale? He asked with no intention to hear more.

"They have an internship, no, coop program. You would never guess where. Guess where?"

"I don't know"

"Make a guess"

"I give up"

"Guess!"

Getting angry, "I give up! I am not going to play along with your childish guessing games. It is either you're going to tell me or not"

"At GM. They usually hire you and send you to college in the program they are affiliated with. That is not the best part, they will pick up the tab"

Taniqua was intrigue and excited for Ketrel, "You're going to do what, learn how to fix cars, sell cars, what is your program called?

"It is called an auto-technician. I will be making big bucks.

Flower Among Ash

I can quit my job at UPS and the cleaning and stay at GM only until I finish my GED. It will take me from now to December to finish the credits and start coop in January '08 at GM. The manager was telling me about it but, then I thought that was an impossible feat until you started talking about school and made it so simple and possible for a person like myself"

"You almost graduated from high school. What happened?"

"A few suspensions"

"Been there too"

"I did not care then. I had a part-time job so making money was all I was interested in back then"

"Are you guys through bonding? We have a job to go to that we are already late for"

"You don't get it. Yes, this is our way out"

Duquan stormed through the door, "I'll wait outside"

"Oh boy. We were arguing before you came in with your big news", Taniqua informed Ketrel.

"He is still not fond of you going back to school?'

"Not at all"

"What are you going to do?

"I already did"

"What?"

"I asked him to move out and I told him with or without him, I am going to college"

"I am happy for you but do you have to break up again. You know he will come running back and."

"Not this time. He does not love me. If he did he would support me. We would get married like mama wanted".

"Why is it you want to get married? Marriage is for old people and statistic shows that people like me and Ingrid who has lived so long in a common-law relation is likely to get a divorce if we get married. I stick with my girl and respect her but that is as far as I will go, well, until I am forty going fifty.

"I admire you running with this. I am proud of you. You are great in my book. I just wish Duquan was more like you towards his children. That dream for us is over Ketrel"

"And I wish Ingrid would be like you, stable and want to get a good education so that one day we can buy a house in Rosedale"

"Rosedale!"

"Yeah Rosedale. You do not think I can buy a house in Rosedale?"

"It is a free country, you can do whatever you want, live wherever you can afford to. At least you have the ambition"

"Well, if not Rosedale, Brampton or Mississauga. Anyway, I should go. I will keep you posted"

"Sure"

Ketrel paused at the door and gave Taniqua a blank stare. "What is it? She whispered. She forced her way passed him and saw Duquan sitting in the hallway with his face wet with tears. She pulled herself back inside as if to hide the fact that she knew he was crying.

"It's your man, you have to talk to him", they whispered to each other.

"He is your best friend; you go talk to him"

"Let's draw straws"

She started to speak loudly. "See you later. Duquan must have gone to the car a long time ago. Oh, there you are. I thought you left"

"Hey D, I forgot my token, give me a minute, or meet me downstairs. Later Taniqua"

Flower Among Ash

"Later. I guess I should get an early nap before DJ gets up. You know how he is demanding"

Duquan got up and stared into her eyes without flinching, "Is this the way you want it? You're going to just kick me out of my home"

"I am not kicking you out. I am tired of living this way and if you won't support me, I have no choice". No matter what, it is going to end up like this"

"The ball is in your court Taniqua. School was the same way. I was never good enough. Nothing I did was every good enough. I gave you my best"

"You gave your best to a Heather, I got the debris. Sorry. As I said before, you can stay until you get a place. I cannot do this anymore"

"Don't say I did not warn you but them teachers that you're so happy to go and sit in their classrooms, they are going to sabotage you. When they do, don't come crying to me when you fail and drop out again".

"At least I tried"

"You are going nowhere out of this jungle sweetheart and I'll be here to say I told you so".

Taniqua was fuming with rage. She shook her head, "Watch me get up out of here and you will be eating my dust". She hurried inside and slammed the door behind her. She curled up at the door as her heartbreaks at the crumbling of her relationship. She covered her mouth with the thought that if Duquan were still outside, he would not hear her sob. She manages to crawled into the sofa where she spent the night looking for the one wishing star in the starry sky through her bare window to wish her anguish away.

She Fell from Great Heights

It was the last weekend of summer. The apartment across the hall was finally rented since the robbery that took the lives of the previous occupants. The perpetrator was never caught. People in this area never seem to see or hear anything. Ironically, the occupants of the building do interact with each in the little parkette, hang out for a smoke, party together, and even have BBQ in the parking lot of the building but still, no one is willing to cooperate with the police.

Looking from the outside of the building, one would ask if life still exists here. The dilapidated building is beyond repair but still its ancient rustic charm attracts many who cannot afford to live elsewhere. The tenants seem complacent to their situation while living their lives disconnected from their harsh reality.

Duquan was coming back from the store. They spend more money in air freshener that on milk for the children. The garbage shoot was close to their apartment and the smell of the overnight garbage would permeate under their door competing with the trash on the outside. He met Ketrel on his way up to his apartment.

From the elevator, they could hear a smoke detector going off. It was quite strange since the building was not up to fire regulation code and no one cared to install a smoke detector in their apartment. As they turned the corner going towards Duquan's apartment, the noise got louder and Duquan raced to his apartment door thinking his apartment was on fire. He struggled trying to find the right key. In his frantic search, he had forgotten he had not installed a smoke detector in the apartment.

Ketrel tapped him on his shoulder and pointed to the apartment across the hall, "It's coming from in there".

The door was ajar that they could see the smoke running along the ceiling. They called out to check if anyone was home. No one answered. They let themselves in when they heard a sob. Duquan made his way to the kitchen and turn off the stove and open the windows and the balcony door. Ketrel was just standing there looking at the woman that was curled up between the refrigerator and the cupboard with her face to the wall.

She had long flowing tinted hair and dressed in a business pantsuit. She was too sorrowful to notice the guys hovering over her.

Ketrel broke the silence," Say something"

Duquan cleared his throat but she did not respond. He cleared his throat a little louder, "Miss, your steak is burning"

Excitedly Ketrel spoke, steak! No one on this building can afford stake. Are you sure it is stake dog? Let me see it! He walked over to the frying pot, "I've never seen cook stake this close. I wonder what it tastes like"

"Burned", Duquan replied sharply then return his attention to the woman crouched over in the corner. "Miss, dinner in done" he said to her.

Ketrel got excited and wondered off, "Wow! Look at the furniture, black leather. That must be a Persian rug they talk about on Tele. I must sit on this; this is a chance of a lifetime. Dog! Pictures on the walls. You only see this in a museum. I wonder how much you can get for this on the streets".

Duquan watched helplessly as Ketrel exploring

Flower Among Ash

the apartment, she stood up and watched with him in amazement.

"A flat screen television mounted on the wall, real plants by the window and drapery! He looked around to the two pairs of eyes watching him. "You must be a goddess or a descendant from the mother-land. A black princess like those in the soap opera, even better and your extensions. Is that real synthetic hair or human hair?".

She spoke softly," It is human hair"

"Store bought. Nice choice of color. It looks good on you".

"I am so drawn to his charm", she told Duquan sarcastically.

"I do not know this person. You're embarrassing me Ketrel".

Ketrel got excited when he saw the goldfish in a huge lit tank. "An aquarium with gold fish, real goldfish moving around. What's up whittle fishy", he greeted the fish and tapped on the glass. "That one is looking at me as if it wants to say something. Do you think fish can talk Duquan? I always wanted a goldfish. What do you want to tell me boy? I am listening." Being mesmerized by the scenery in the aquarium he asked, "Didn't I sound like Fraser when I said, I am listening". He imitated the TV character. "Wow! God made these little fish. I always thought God has gigantic hands. It would take a small hand to make little fish like these. They are saying something, I know it. I am picking up a signal, it is wavy and floating in the water. Wow!"

Getting back to the situation at hand, "Don't pay him any attention. The grass got to his head. I told you that your head is too light for pot. Back to you, Are you ok? Come into the living-room and sit for a while, you seem distress when we got here". They walked over to the sofa while Ketrel amuses himself with the fish. Duquan tried to comfort their new neighbor, "How does a classy babe like yourself end up in a place like this. Sit. What happened?

"Life. One-minute I am on top, the next minute my corporate world crashes. I tried to keep up with the Jones' but I was only living a lie. I thought of selling all my furniture but they are the only things I have that gives me hope and reminds me of life when things were good"

Ketrel interrupted, "The big fall from corporate Canada. How can you have faith in furniture? If I were you I would sell them and rent a roach free motel. Where you live make a better impression on your friends. So, are you going to invite them to your slum?

"Heck no!"

"You are one of us now. You're acting like you are all that"

"You are assuming Ketrel", she replied

"It looks like you chose to come down here because this is your old stomping ground. How the mighty have fallen", Ketrel continued.

"I must apologize for my friend; he is never like this, rude. Is my psychic telling the truth; you are from the hood? How did you get up to corporate Canada?"

"I mimic and imitate my rich white friends. I played the game in school, playing up to the professor….

"Kissing up? Duquan questioned her as if he understood exactly what she was talking about. "I was too proud to kiss up to my teachers and besides, I was always in the wrong. They hated the way I dressed, the way I spoke and the way I looked. My Jamaican accent is strong and they put me in all the ESL classes with the Chinese students. When they were there speaking their language, I sat there thinking to myself, I understand English so why was I in the same class with them? It is my first language but it was not good enough and so I suffered. I on the other hand was too stressed to play up to my teachers. They could not relate to me"

"What are you talking about? You are as crazy as your friend. I am talking about the cooperate world and you are rambling about elementary school. Are you for real? She questioned in astonishment.

"You must have reached the top because your furniture does not look like anything I've seen in this building. I would advise you to put chains on the door and keep it lock. Burglars go from building to building to case the place and then return at night or when you are out to rob you", Duquan informed her. "Do you have a fan so I can blow the rest of the smoke out of the apartment", he continued.

"Why were you crying earlier? Ketrel interjected.

"I swore never to come back to this stink hole and here I am. I tried hard, very hard and it all came crashing down; even my friends became too busy for me. I could not keep up with the fancy restaurants and going on cruises. They had rich parents and trust funds while I have a road sweeper for a father. My mom, a housekeeper. I was so embarrassed. I told my friends I live in a boarding home while my parents were travelling to Kenya, South Africa or other place in Europe on business trips and vacations. They were always away".

"And they were always here. Duquan, what if my little girl grows up to be embarrassed about me. That would be hurtful after I worked so hard to take care of her", Ketrel inquired.

"If your girl tries something like that, Ingrid would give them her Jamaican history and some fine native style wake up call. Put joke aside, how did your parents react to your attitude?"

"I did not care", she replied.

"You're selfish", Ketrel added.

"The pot calling the kettle black, eh Duquan"

"Welcome to the neighborhood, get reacquainted. C'mon Ketrel. She is alright, let's go"

"Watch your back with all this high-priced furniture. For peace of mind, get rid of them"

"You guys don't get it"

Duquan partly empathizing with her, "We understand the struggle but you went too far lying about your parents like that. Anyways, it's water under the bridge. We all make mistakes some way along life's journey. I don't know what else to say but keep it real and I wish you all the best. Welcome to the neighborhood again"

"I won't be here for long. If there is a way out of this stink hole and I will find it again. I refuse to live here for long", she assures them.

"We didn't expect to be here forever but it is our home, respect it. At least you're not homeless", Ketrel added. "This is just a passage girl. Things will get better but stop denying this. You go out there to run with the Jones and you will see how fast you come back down here"

"This is it. Not another time"

Ketrel sat beside her, "You have been here before and

Flower Among Ash

you've not learned from your mistakes. I bet you're still in denial. And the furniture?

"I had this furniture from my first promotion. They are a symbol of my success and who I am"

"They are also a symbol of your failure. What if one day this place is not here or there was no vacancy? What if the next fall lands you on the street, will you go to your mama then", Ketrel questioned her rhetorically.

"C'mon dog. Have a good day madam"

"Good day. What is your name?"

"Robin"

"The one your mama gave you", Ketrel insisted.

"Kenya and yes, like the country"

"The sad thing about this is you are ashamed of your roots. Look in the mirror lady. A leopard cannot change its spots. Have a good day".

Misconception

Flower Among Ash

Taniqua decided on picking up Tanisha from school because of the bruises that she came home with on her legs and hands. Despite her numerous complaints to the supervisor, nothing was done to separate her daughter from the aggressive child that was constantly in conflict with Tanisha. Taniqua was in rage and planned on taking the bull by the horn to stop the incidents that caused the bruises on her daughter's hands and feet.

Mrs. Harrison was on the steps talking to another parent when she got there. Mrs. Harrison looked at her and continued to make small talk with the other parents while purposely ignoring Taniqua.

Taniqua approached her and interrupted their conversation with the parent, "Mrs. Harrison; I would like to speak to you. It is urgent"

Mrs. Harrison looked at her and continued with the conversation. A few second later Tanisha darted out of the building to greet her mother but Taniqua was too preoccupied waiting for Mrs. Harrison to explain to her why the incidents have not stopped.

"Where is auntie Ingrid mom? Why are you picking me up and not her? Tanisha kept on speaking but her words fell on deaf ears.

"Mrs. Harrison, I said I would like to speak with you, now! please" Taniqua demanded. The other parent excused himself and left the two of them standing there in dead silence for the longest three seconds until Mrs. Harrison finally spoke.

"Go home and take care of your children. Should you want to speak to me, please make an appointment with my secretary", she informed Taniqua.

She was about to re-enter the school when Taniqua blocked the doorway. "You have been ignoring my notes all week but you are not going to ignore me now. Why haven't you stop the boy from hurting my child? I have asked you to separate them so she would not come home bruised and still you did nothing. I am expecting this to stop as of today"

"Who do you think you are talking to? Why don't you take the responsibility and talk to your child about staying away from trouble"? she answered angrily. "I am not going to argue with you. Don't speak to me in that manner", she continued feeling insulted.

"Tanisha is your responsibility when she is in your classroom! This boy kept on picking on my daughter and you just sit there and do noting about it"

"It is just like your kind to blame everybody else for your problem. If you did not want the responsibility of caring for a child, then you should not have…

"Do not even go there"

"Go where?

"I know how you people think of me…

"Remarkable! I must apologize for not being able to talk to you on your level because you are now assuming how I think from an unfinished statement"

"Mrs. Harrison, I have asked you a thousand times to keep them apart. Why haven't you?

Mrs. Harrison sends Tanisha to play in the sand-box so she could speak to her mother. When she was out of earshot she unleashes on Taniqua. "I got your notes. They were all written in a very distasteful manner, they were also illegible and disrespectful".

"That is a lie; they were typed".

Flower Among Ash

"That is beside the point. You are getting hysterical and outrage at me when you are the problem"

"You are the teacher; you are creating the problem by not separating the boy from my daughter. It is called classroom management. YES! I said it. I know a thing or two about creating a safe classroom climate of which you and your staff are not doing".

"Is that all you know? I am going to be frank. Tanisha has not grasp the concept that when a relationship is not working or is causing harm, she should sever said relationship. Look at yourself for instance. How many children you have feeding off government's money and you have not stopped. You're a prime example of someone in a relationship and do not know when to cut ties when its not working".

Taniqua was now outraged. "This is not about me or her father, which is none of your business. Let me tell you something; if I had not known the Lord, you would not have heard the last of this for that comment"

"Gee! Jesus does saves! Keep your paranoia to yourself. The child is just role playing what she sees at home"

"Her father does not hit me"

"Tell it to Dr. Phil. Good day!

"This is not over"

"Please get out of my way and go and sit down with your daughter before she ends up like you. And as they say; like mother, like daughter which is the trigger to all this"

Taniqua got out of her way, "I am going to report you to …

"To whom, my husband, who is the owner to this fine establishment. This is my place of business. If you do not like it take your child to a more private school which I know you cannot afford. F.Y. I. Dollar DAZ are going on at No Frills. The sale ends today. You might want to run along and get some marked down groceries", she told her scornfully and disappeared into the school.

Taniqua shouted after her, "don't judge me because of my situation. You should be more accepting and understanding of a family instead of ridiculing and acting like a snob to the unfortunate. You didn't feel this way towards us when you were cashing the voucher. Only people like me register their children in your so-called fine establishment".

"Whatever makes you sleep at night dear", she answered back.

Taniqua was still bothered about her conversation with Mrs. Harrison. She was still fuming while she made dinner for her children. No one was there for her to vent to. She started banging the pots and mumbling to herself when the phone rang. It was Ingrid.

"Hello. Just cleaning up some dishes and making dinner. I'm glad that you called. I am so upset about what happened at Tanisha' daycare. Mrs. Harrison is something else. I guess I should have let you deal with it. I am sick and tired of this.

"Of what?

"Isn't it obvious. The way people think of me as if… Hmmm… I know I should not let her get to me but I cannot help it. I am not strong like you and I think she is right in some way".

"Don't let her get to you. She is just a miserable woman who wants everyone to be frustrating as her. Calm down Taniqua".

"You are right, and she had the nerve to say that Tanisha is going to be just like me having lots of children in an abusive relationship. She claims that Tanisha is the one messing with the boy. She basically is treating her like dirt because of the way she sees me and where I live", she said trying to piece her words together.

"I tell you to let me deal with it but you're not listening to me. She can't get in my head because I am proud of who I am. I do not care what other people think of me. You are too concern about what other people think. Stop being ashamed of who you are".

"And by the way, she had the nerve to tell me that No Frills has sales and that I need to go get groceries while the sale last as if she is working with the company".

"That is to show you that she shops there too. Let it go Taniqua. I meant to go by there to pick up a few snacks. We could go together when Duquan gets home".

"Speaking of the devil. He just walked in".

"Meet me in the lobby".

Duquan, Ingrid and I are going shopping. Watch the children until I return. I won't be long. They have eaten their dinner so they will not be hungry. They are not going to daycare tomorrow so they can watch TV or you can read to them. DJ is sleeping. He did not eat before he went to bed so feed him if he wakes up".

"I am their father; you don't have to give me all those details. I know how to take care of my children"

"Whatever you say".

"I am giving you one hour.

"And if..

"Don't bother with that; I have people to see and places to go"

His comment fuels her anger, "Why don't you go away.

I am going to get groceries for our children and you are timing me before I get to the door! GO Duquan! I do not need this!

"Don't start anything with me. I have no time for this"

"You have no time. Say you have no time for your children. That's what's up"

"There you go again, putting words in my mouth".

"I do not have to put words into your mouth because you are hardly ever here"

"I am here now"

"WHOOPEEE! for me"

"Are you going or not?

Just then Ingrid walked through the open door, "Lets go"

"In a minute', Taniqua replied.

"Duquan, you just got here, what is it with you two? Gosh", Ingrid added.

"It is she who is starting something with me as usual" he tried to explain himself when he was interrupted.

Taniqua got her purse and started for the door, "He does not want to stay with his own children. He claimed he has more important things to do. It is not like he is giving me the money for the grocery. Today is just not my day".

"I don't know what is going on with you two but Taniqua, you need to relax. You are too easily wound up. Be satisfied with whom you are. Too much drama. Let's go and maybe if you are a good girl I'll take you to Mandarin for take out", she said jokingly.

Well Oiled Plan

Flower Among Ash

Although the store was closed at nine PM; Taniqua did not come home until after midnight. She stopped by Ingrid's and watched the movie, "21". Her intention was deliberate, to keep Duquan home with the children. She was expecting him to be in a rage when she got home but when she got there, the house was empty. She called Ketrel to find out if he knew of Duquan's whereabouts, but he did not pick up either. Her mother was at work, so she knew that the children were not there. After calling all the possible place they could have been; the door opened.

Before he could push his head through the door; Taniqua started the interrogation. "Where have you been? Don't you see how late it is?"

"Please help me with the children", he said to her politely. "Take the twins stroller and let me put DJ down. Tanisha is coming slowly behind me. You know how she does it; sleep walking".

When all the children were tucked in bed, Duquan went and showered. Taniqua was a bit disappointed that he was not home waiting for her and getting upset because she stayed out late. He said nothing and she assumed he was not aware of the fact that she was also out late. Her well oiled plan had failed.

Duquan came out of the shower in his boxers and towel drying his unbraided Afro. "Do me a favor please"

"What?

"My hair"

"Don't you see what time it is?

"You're not sleeping"

"But I am sleepy"

"You're not in bed"

"Ok"

"Where is the comb?

"It has no teeth"

"What do you mean it has no teeth? What do you use to comb Tanisha's hair?

"Tanisha's tough woolly hair broke out all the teeth. Her hair is just like her daddy's"

"And charismatic like her daddy too"

"Whatever gets you through the day"

"Isn't that the reason why you fell for me?

"And falling was never a good thing"

"What does that mean?

"Nothing"

"Are you going to braid my hair before it dries and get knotted?

"Get a comb and I will do it".

"Where is it?

"It is somewhere on the dresser in the bedroom, whatever left of it"

Duquan went and got the half broken comb and showed it to her. "Is this it? I guess this will do".

"Because you are not the one doing the combing. Hurry up! I want to go to my bed. I have no time for this"

"Don't talk to me like that; like you're talking to your child".

"If you were my child", she spoke under her breath.

"What?

"Are you coming or not?

"Did you do my laundry? I need a shirt"

"What am I to you; your maid? I am going to bed", she said a headed for the bedroom.

Flower Among Ash

"OK! Here is the comb"

She sat back down on the sofa and she started to braiding his hair when he suggested them watching a movie. He got up before she could have finished the first cornrow. He was having problems operating the VCR. "This is not working"

"Use the knife"

"To do what?

"To turn on the VCR". She got up and pushed him out of the way and got the movie started and went back to doing his hair.

"You need to throw that out"

"It still has good use to the children"

"Have you ever heard of a DVD player?

"Get me one. This VCR you want me to throw out was the first birthday gift you gave me that was valuable back then. I may have to use a kitchen knife to operate it but it is what I have for now".

"Sentimental"

"I did not say that"

"You do not need the VCR when you have the real deal". She tugged on his hair.

"OOCH! I am just saying that you are holding on to this crap when you can have all of this"

"Holding on this piece of crap; I could say that about you"

"That was low"

"Well, do not dis my VCR. Turn your head the other way. I am the mother of your children and you are acting as if you're a gift to me and our children than a mate and a father"

"I am just not ready for…

"I was not ready for this either but I have to live with it.

You can come and go when you get tired of being a parent but I cannot. Lucky, you!" she interjected.

"It is not like that. I am here when I can"

"Did you get the message from the agency?

"Yes but I am not working for no nine dollars per hour"

She was annoyed and gripped his hair tighter. "Look at me! You have no skills or degree so take what you get until something better comes along. You do that with your women, why not work. He fought to get out of her grip. "Look! Today I had to ruffle through spoiled produced to feed your children and you cannot commit to working a job that would make your children eat better. What would I have done without the dollar bargain at the grocery store? Is it because I did not take you to court?

"Go ahead and take me to court; you know what you would get? NOTHING!

"So that is the reason why you do not want to get a real job. When you get caught selling drugs again, do not call me"

"I did not hold you down and got you pregnant. You wanted me just as bad as I wanted you so don't put this all on me"

"Good night Duquan! She went into the bedroom and she slammed the door behind her.

Duquan stood there talking to himself while making himself comfortable in the sofa for the night. "One of these days those hinges are going to come apart, slamming door on me. Acting as if I forced this on her. I am not taking the blame for this alone. I am a free spirit person. You will never tame this man. No woman is going to tie me down. Goodnight to you too".

What Now!

Flower Among Ash

Taniqua walked into the apartment listlessly after a long day trying to complete the registration process at school. Her expression showed a day that was going wrong. She puts the children down to sleep and checked the messages on her answering machine. Her hopeless sighs were trigger from an exasperating ordeal taking care of the children and trying to move forward with her life.

Duquan still lived at the apartment but he made himself unavailable for her and the children. In the summer humidity, she had to carry all four children with her as she explored the possibilities to be enrolled in college and change the direction of her life.

She had become depressed and disappointed. The news about her children's father affair made it unbearable for her. She would lock herself into the bedroom when he was home and most times cried herself to sleep. She wanted to give up. All the chaos caused more confusion for her.

A few days later, closer to the deadline she picked up the telephone and called the college again. "I am returning Allison Rodriguez's call. Hi Allison it's Taniqua, you left a message saying that I should call you as soon as possible".

"The ECE program? I am willing to try anything at this moment".

"There is a demand for ECE and you can even open your own daycare in the future", she explained.

"How long does the ECE program will last?

"Two years and one year for the intensive", she continued.

"I just wanted to make a change in my life. I am at the fork in the road. I am not sure if I want to become an Early Childhood Educator. What about a dental assistance?

"If that is what you prefer. You will need to complete the prerequisite courses", she added.

"What about the tuition", Taniqua asked.

"OSAP is available. You would have to apply immediately. Did you complete the application for the school?

"I did", Taniqua answered.

"Wait a bit. It seems as if you've been accepted. Did you get the information for your courses and text books information?

"No".

"Have you been on Blackboard?

"No", Taniqua answered not knowing exactly what Mrs. Rodriguez was talking about. "Why don't you come on campus and I'll help you with the procedure".

"I will. Thank you so much. See you tomorrow", she replied joyfully.

She called Ingrid immediately disregarding the time. "You will never guess what just happened? I got accepted into George Brown. I am going to school!

"Taniqua, do you know what time it is? Ingrid asked half awake.

"I had to share the good news with my besties! Tomorrow I am going there to make it final. I did it!

"Good for you", Ingrid said without enthusiasm.

"I thought you'd be happy for me Ingrid".

"This is what you got me up for? She questioned Taniqua angrily. "I don't want to hear anything more about you or school from you and Ketrel. Goodnight", she told Taniqua and hang up the phone.

"Ok. Goodnight to you too".

Where are my Books?

Taniqua wanted to celebrate her first month anniversary in school. Duquan was home when she got there. She wanted to go out with Ketrel and Ingrid.

"Where are the kids?" Duquan asked.

"With my mom, she is going to drop them off after they have supper. Where have you been? you did not give me your new phone number", Duquan inquired.

"You live here, occasionally, I don't need to give you anything"

"Are you ignoring me?"

"I am talking to you, aren't I?"

"Why can't you look at me instead of burying your face into your textbooks. I guess since you are now going back to school, you'll feel like you're better than me".

"So why did you ask me where I was today when you knew I was at school. I have no time for this, leave me alone".

"How am I suppose to get in touch with you in case of emergency and what if I want to talk to the kids?"

"You're full of questions today! Well Duquan, last time I check you were living in this living room, you come and go as you like, so, what's the problem?

"How you got the phone hooked up?"

"I borrowed money from Ketrel".

"Strange" he replied in disbelief.

"What's so strange about that?".

"Both of you decided to go back to school, then you got back the phone, you tell me what's strange about this. Did he give you a cell phone too?".

"It was a package deal and it is a loan. I am going to

repay him as soon as I receive my OSAP loan. Whatever you are insinuating, don't".

"Feeling guilty".

"As I recall, the last time Ingrid signed you up for a family plan with Rogers and you got a free phone, what was that all about?".

"That was different".

"How different?".

"I have no time for this".

"Really. You are the one who is bugging and tripping up all over yourself. I have better things to do".

"Assignments".

"Did Ketrel bought you your books because I only have half of the rent and it was due a week ago; I hope you were not relying on me to buy your books or buy metro pass. I told you, you are not college material. Very soon you will drop out and then people will be laughing at you. Why bother"

"Are you done with your speech? It has been a month since I started school and I am doing fine without you so far. I am not going to get angry with you. If you had not done something like that, I would be concern. I applied for welfare"

"You on welfare. I thought that was beneath you and now that you're a college student"

"I will do whatever it takes to get me through school".

"OK! I will keep my money".

"Excuse you. I did not get it yet and ……why are you doing this to me? You hate me that much".

"I told you I will not stand by while you go on to a better life"

"So that's what's up. It is a free country. I am not stopping you from making something of yourself and besides, Ketrel taking me out to celebrate later".

"You are so lucky that your mother got laid off to watched the kids; it's like how things always worked out in the Soap Opera; because I was not going to spend all day watching them while you are out having a wonderful time".

Screaming on the top of her lungs and the tears gushing from her eyes. Her words broke up as she speaks like a telephone that dropping calls. "I am at school studying! And they are your children! I've been through this with you and I am not going to do this again. I cannot believe that I have having this argument with you again. You want to leave me permanently, then go. Please go! I've had enough. You brought up Ketrel as an excuse to leave. You do not need any excuse to leave, just go. And by the way, I know about miss Lexus. I saw you in the car. You seem to be fascinated with blonds. What are you, her pool boy, her boy toy, what? She is probably old enough to be your mother because your mother looks much better than her and another thing, you cannot tell me that she is telling you to break up your family. Let me tell you this, one day she is going to put you out like the stale garbage you are because they are progressive people and certainly will not entertain you when she sees your true color. But, I forget, men like you when you're with the other woman climb Mount Everest for them but for your children, oh no! Get out! Get out now!"

Duquan reached in the corner for his already packed duffle bags.

"I cannot believe I fell into your trap. Why didn't you just leave. It wouldn't have matter. You needed no excuse.

You brought up things that are all insinuation just to have a reason to leave, you said all the right words to let me kick you out. Now Duquan, you've got legitimate reasons to leave, go. I will survive. I always do."

"Here is the half of the rent. You do not deserve it but anyway, buy some grocery". He threw the money on the sofa and took up his things and left.

The phone rang. It was Ingrid. She broke down. "He left for good this time Ingrid. Duquan is gone and he is never coming back. He wanted to leave all along. All I did was love him and have his children. Now I have nothing. I still love him. Probably if I drop out of school, you know, he will come back and I have all this homework and I don't have all my books yet. I still need a few more books immediately. Are you there? She asked.

Ingrid broke her silence. "Can you not pick up the phone without the drama and books?

"I am sorry to be venting on you. Its just the anxiety and uncertainty. What if Duquan is right?

"There you go again. Can I not have a conversation with you like we used to?

"I am so sorry for missing girls' night the other day. I had three assignments due the next day. Tanisha and Raven were disappointed", Taniqua explained.

"Instead of getting frantic about books and assignments, why not study at the library there? You're the smart one".

"You have every right to be upset but you need to understand that I have to complete all my assignments and get a good grade to stay in school", Taniqua explained.

"Are you working hard to prove Duquan wrong"

"You know better. I am doing this for me so I can

move out of this dump and have a better life. I need to take better care of my children and not having people like Mrs. Harrison at the daycare", she rambled on.

"Ok. Whatever. I called you to remind you about the children's playdate later. I already bought the burgers, hot dogs, ice cream, and you were suppose to bring the juice, dessert, and movie".

"I remembered. My mother will be dropping them off at your place. She hates taking the elevator. I'll come over then".

"Whatever you say. Later".

When the Water Recedes

Flower Among Ash

The door was unlocked and hearing the loud sobbing, Robin let herself in. Before she could say a word, Taniqua yelled at her to leave. Shortly Ketrel came in with some books from the library. He spent some time with her, comforting her. On his way, he noticed that Robin was moving out of the building. She updated him with the changes in her situation. She tried to find out what was going on with Taniqua when Taniqua came to the door and saw them standing there. "Sorry about that earlier", she apologized to Robin.

"I wanted to let you know that I was moving and to ask you if you wanted any of my stuff. Most of the electronics are sold except for the living room and dining room sets plus the day bed and a few other things. Come in if you're interested. I don't want to be rude but your furniture looks like something you purchase from the flea market dump. They are tacky"

"The Salvation Army and Goodwill, more like it" Taniqua corrected her.

"That is disgusting. You have no taste at all!"

"Moving out already? Ketrel interjected"

"And not a day later. This place would make me suicidal if I had to sleep in this dump another night. I am not cut out for poverty and this morbid way of life".

"Good for you; what was your name? Taniqua asked.

"Kenya, the country, otherwise know as Robin", Ketrel answered. "You have not met your neighbor!

"I don't think so", Taniqua replied.

"I've been here for just a short time. It felt as if I was doing time but that is behind me now. I am moving on up out of here"

"Good for you. It has been a dream of mine but some

of us have no better place to live but here; you know what I'm saying", Ketrel added.

"Speak for yourself", Robin replied rudely. "So Mr. Ketrel, what do you think of me now? Weeping was for that one day you and your friend saw me but my joy came today. How do you like me now?

"Are you going back to your black mother or are you still denying your blackness?

"I will not dignify that with an answer but what you can do is to help your friend haul the things she needs and get rid of her junk. Other than that, you are out of my league boy".

"Out of my league", Ketrel repeated. "Yet for a few months we lived in the same apartment, lived in the same community, drank the same sewer water, inhale that same garbage; what do you have to say about that?

"It was just a minor set back"

Taniqua eyes was caught on the furniture and made her way into the apartment. "I like your leather sofa, is that the day bed? It would be great for Tanisha. I could put it in the living room. That little table would be perfect but I don't have a dime!"

"It is yours", Robin answered feeling as if she has arrived.

"You're giving them to her for free?!"

"Sure! Why not. Her life seems to be going downhill with all the brawl I heard coming from the apartment"

"Sorry for the disturbance", Taniqua apologized.

"Another thing, hearing your sad story through the keyhole, I can give you my last month rent, since I have to move out suddenly. I was living on a month-to-month lease because I had no hope of making this permanent"

"So you're a peeping Tom too fake lady?"

"Ketrel! I am getting some free stuff here, chill!"

"Anyway I will tell the manager to do that and you can have only the large sofa with the other things you want"

While they were switching furniture the manager and the super came by. They talked about Robin's rent and agreed to transfer the last month's rent to Taniqua's apartment. They all volunteered to take the old furniture outside while Taniqua sweep up to make room for her seemingly brand new used furniture. Ketrel rolled in a twenty-five-inch flat screen television on a TV stand while she was cleaning up.

"Quick! Hide this in the bedroom!"

"What are you doing Ketrel?"

"It was in the bedroom. She doesn't want it"

"I can't steal from her; she practically giving me anything I want plus my rent. This is dishonest", Taniqua rebuked him.

"It is not like she was not going to give it to you"

"But I did not tell her that I was going to take it. She gave me what I asked for"

"Your TV shows Sponge Bob in black and white. Your children do not know the color, the true color of Sponge Bob. I am looking out for you", Ketrel argued.

"I know but I have to tell her. What if it was already sold? I better catch her before she leaves"

"What if she says no?"

"Then I'll have to give it back"

"I was looking out for you".

"I want it the honest way. Look at my life. I cannot take anymore bad luck in my life. I appreciate you looking out for me but we have to be honest"

She went to Robin's apartment and explained that Ketrel had taken some stuff by mistake. Robin told her she could have the television and gave her a few kitchen appliances extra. Taniqua had finished arranging her new used furniture when Robin came in to say goodbye.

"What are you going to do now? Where will you live"

"I am a living-in babysitter"

Ketrel was stunned, "What! A babysitter? You!"

"I have a plan. If I keep the apartment, I would have to come here on weekends but if I have no apartment, I will be able to stay there with my new family 24/7"

"Why would you want to do that? Taniqua asked looking a bit confused.

"The wife does her charity work on weekends and I have to go out to luncheons and sometimes dinner with the father and the brats; her children. From the description of my work, I will be having lots of luncheons outside the home with the father and some evenings I will be at the house alone with my future husband"

"Home wrecker; that is disgusting! The poor woman does not see the hurricane that is heading her way. All through the interview you were listening for the opportunity to break up a perfect family. What is wrong with you? Is it so bad to live here that you must hurt some innocent children to get what you want? That is so nasty!", Ketrel reprimanded her.

"Who said they are perfect? It is just another opportunity for me to step up out of here. Beside he wanted to kiss me, unfortunately, he missed my lips. I am going to have his baby; he is going to purchase a condo for me and my illegitimate child and eventually he will leave her and marry me but if not, it's a win-win situation because I will be living off his hush money with my son in a brand-new condo. It does not matter what you think of me because I am the one that is leaving you all in my dust".

"You're crazy. You need a reality check. What you need to do like us real folks, is to go back to school, get a career and stand on your own two feet instead of sleeping your way to the top. Have you not learned from your past mistake? It got you coming back to the ghetto. What if it happens again?"

"It won't. This is a full proof plan"

"What are you going to do, drug the man?"

"Got to go. See you, wouldn't want to be yah", she said and left them standing there looking dazed.

She left Taniqua in a bewildered state of mind. She was ambiguous as what to do, should she give back the furniture so her plan will fail or accept it as none of her business. She had taken furniture from a woman whose plot was to destroy someone's family. Her family was just broken by a woman like her and now she is making it easier for Robin to carry out her plan. She thought to herself, "She was going to do it anyway. After all, she was selling her stuff. Whether I took the furniture she was going to break up an innocent family". At the end of the day she had her rent and a new living room. It was a sign of hope for her and the children. She sat alone in the dark after the children had gone to bed, and thought of how she could have done things differently to prevent Duquan from leaving. She looked at her daughter sleeping on the daybed; Tanisha is the mirror image of her father and a constant reminder of him. "I guess it is just us now" she whispered.

Movie and a Blankie

Flower Among Ash

Ingrid has been a support for Taniqua through her roller coaster relationship with Duquan despite her feelings towards her about going to school. She brought over some children's movie and popcorn for them to spend time together.

"Ingrid, I appreciate you hanging out with us tonight", Taniqua told her.

"Because you're my girl. I do not know what I would do if I was with a man like Duquan. No, let me change that statement; if I were you; he would be a converted man, in my church. I would give him my ten commandments; you know what I am saying? To put all joking aside and I do not want to kick you while you're down but God gave me one of the good one when He gave me Ketrel. At first, I did not like him, but after I found out I was pregnant; I said, why not"

"The popcorn is ready; put in the video", Taniqua told her not giving much to what she was saying.

"The button is not working on the remote. The battery must be dead"

"Neither one work. I use the knife"

"A knife? Ingrid asked in disbelief. "What do you have against DVD?

"CASH!"

"You come and do this"

Taniqua got up and got the movie started, "This is the primitive style", she laughed.

"Nah! Primitive people used a REMOTE control"

"Duquan bought it for me for my birthday when we first started dating", she replied.

"Sentimental value?

"Not really. I just cannot afford another one" Taniqua answered.

"DVD players are cheap. They say men are from Mars but sometimes I wonder about you. You must treat yourself with fine things"

"I got some fine furniture"

"I meant that you actually bought for yourself. I have children and that does not stop me from treating myself. Did you pawn your jewelry?

"No. They are somewhere about the place".

"I make time for MOI! Because I am a baby mama, that does not mean that I should carry myself looking like a bag lady; and besides, as the Pastor would say, God's children should be the head and not the tail"

"What are you talking about? The Pastor was leaning towards that believers should represent God in the way we dress; unlike you, I must add".

"Don't be a hater Taniqua! I look good and you know it"

"I am not disputing that but you dress skimpy for a so call believer who do not like to go to church unless it's a holiday"

"What are you now, the fashion police? The fact is, you're looking like an old lady and that is not Godlike"

"Amazing how you can insert God where it suits you"

"God is flexible", Ingrid replied jokingly.

"Back to what you were saying earlier"

"Are we going to watch the movie anytime soon?

"We can watch the movie and talk and besides, it is not like if you have to return them tomorrow", Taniqua continued.

"I have not seen this one yet", Ingrid said trying to evade any further serious talk with Taniqua.

"Ingrid, don't avoid me", Taniqua insisted.

"Isn't watching the movie why we are here; at least why I am here?

"I fell in love with Duquan before we slept together".

"That is the mistake you made Taniqua"

"What?

"You fell. Falling was never a good thing. Look at you two now"

"I couldn't be without him unless I felt something. I wanted to wait until marriage but….

"Don't let me choke on your *No Name* grape punch. That was the olden days. Nobody is waiting these days"

"Tristan said she waited"

"That is what she told you"

"How would you know?

"I got contacts"

"I thought I was your girl. How did I not know about this?

"Taniqua, you're trying to be squeaky clean in your miserable life. Sorry, you can't have your feet on both side of the fence. That is not helping. You live in the ghetto and you do not want to live here. You want back your baby daddy and you want to recommit to God. You are neither here or there. I say, cut your lost and move on"

"Wow Ingrid, you sure lay it on thick"

"You asked"

"And I had to. You make some sense but what man in their right mind would want to be with me, a mother of four"

"That is the wrong way to look at things. You are not looking for a man to settle down with; just someone to make you happy, pay the bills; you know what I'm saying?

"I cannot live like that before my children"

"Who said you have to do anything before your children? Why do you think they build hotels?

"I meant that lifestyle"

"It is the Christian thing, isn't it"?

"It is not like Duquan and I are married or that he will one day ask me to marry him. He is not the marrying type. He is more of a rolling stone that gather no moss type, but I know people waited before they got married and statistic says a relationship will last if you do not have sex with your partner prior to marriage".

Ingrid interrupter her, "Let me stop you there! That is for people getting married. It is said that a couple should be friends first and leave the sex till the wedding night. Be real now. Our baby daddies are not going to marry us and who say I want to anyway?

"If Ketrel asked you, wouldn't you?

"Are you not listening to me? No"

"You're kidding"

"Also my friend that lived together for a while and then got married are now separated. How'd you like them apples?

"So it does not bother you?

Tanisha was getting restless. "Go for your blankie"

Tanisha walked to the kitchen table for her blankie and came back and snuggled in her mother's lap. "Is daddy coming home tonight mama?

"I am not mama, grandmother is mama, I am mommy. Daddy is coming when you get into bed like Santa. He is working late baby" she told Tanisha withholding the sad truth of her reality.

"PEW! Your blankie smells Tanisha"

"Nah huh!

"You let her walk around with a blankie? She is five going on to be six years old"

"It comforts her especially when her dad has to work late"

Ingrid tried hard not to blurt out the truth. "Do you think that this is healthy to have her depending on a blankie for comfort?

"He means the world to her", Taniqua said while reassuring her daughter.

Ingrid held her nose as the dingy smell from the blankie reached her, "Put that in the garbage. Taniqua, you got to let your little girl grow up"

"No one complained about Gandhi and his blankie"

"I agree with you, but those were sheets", she chuckled.

Carbon Footprint

Taniqua got another predictable call from her mother. The one that is triggered by an unrelated death of a stranger in Toronto. The victim was Tamara. A young single mother gunned down in her apartment by angry gang members who wanted revenge. They broke into the house and killed her in front of her children. The horrific news resulted into another invitation to church. Taniqua did not argue with her mother because she knew her relentlessness and persistence would become the haunting she could not endure.

She was still asleep when the church van came to pick her up. She slept in longer until the driver gave up waiting on her and left. The frequent interval of phone calls from her mother were enough grenade to get her out of the apartment. When she arrived at the church she took the children to the basement for children's church and then joined the service in the main sanctuary. She entered the sanctuary in time to hear the mother of the slain girl pouring her heart out to the congregation. She then realized and understood the profound effect this had on her mother because she too was raised in the church and had left the church. Taniqua was too mesmerized with her story to look for a seat in the crowded pews. She leaned against the wall while soaking up the information like a sponge.

"I remembered how thrilled she was to be an adventurer. We never missed not one event. Pathfinder was another proud moment for us. Each year she would get so many honors even to the point of getting me involved. Learning to tie knots and how to start a camp fire was adventurous for us. She wanted to become a master guide but she got pregnant. My carbon footprint on her life changed from that day until the day she died. I was like many of you who did not use the opportunities we had to love her back to Christ. I ask myself every day, what legacy did I passed on to her. She died thinking that God is unforgiving and cold and that once you made a mistake you can never come back to Him. By the time I realized how badly I had misrepresented God, it was too late. She was expecting another child and has gotten so far in that lifestyle that she had no desire to return to God. My carbon footprint on her life cost her the gift of salvation. I was not the only one to blame. As a single mother, and I am not making any excuse, I was expecting my church family to be that village that would help me raise my little girl. Instead, the wolves in sheep clothing that we all trusted came over to help me move into our new apartment and used that opportunity to develop a relationship with my daughter. I thought he was just being nice to us. Being there when I needed a friend. His legacy and carbon footprint on my child was a child which led her in having other relationships. God wants the wheat and tears to grow together until the time of harvest, but, for how long? The carbon footprint that we left on her we can never undo, is a false characteristic of who God truly is and she died not knowing that. She needed a father figure in her life and he, the responsible adult, took advantage of her vulnerability. She does not have a second chance to eternal life, I prayed she had prayed the sinner prayer before her breath returned to God, if not, she is lost forever and I am stuck with regret because unlike her, I do not have another chance to ask her to forgive me or to tell her the truth about God. That God loves her and has never stopped loving her. I asked God to forgive me and I know He has but, it would have been better if I could say those words to her. I loved her and it pains my heart with such deep regret that I messed up so badly as a mother. I am pleading to all single mothers in this church not to put your trust in men regardless of the office they have in church. You have some wonderful converted Christian men here but there are a few wolves in sheep's clothing that cannot be trusted. These men preys on single women with the pretense of coming to your rescue in your time of need. Be vigilant and keep a close watch on your little girls and please love your children back into the church. I see Taniqua standing there in the back. I want you to know that God loves you and your mother wants what is best for you. Your mother and I have been friends forever since she brought me into the church. Please do not let what happened to Tamara happen to you. I am asking for your prayers and support for my family and Tamara's children and siblings.

The pastor walked up to the pulpit and placed his hand across her shoulders. "We are here for you sister Suzie. We feel your pain. She was a part of this church family regardless. I will closely work with a few elders and deaconesses to assist you in your time of bereavement. Let us pray", he addressed the congregation and then he offered a word of prayer.

Taniqua sat next to her mother after the touching testimony from sister Suzie. She could not get sister Suzie's words out of her mind with her mother's added narration. She excused herself and went to join the children in children's church. The atmosphere was less intense. She stayed there until the end of the service and slipped out before her mother and friends caught up to her. That did not prevent her mother from dropping in on her unannounced with a half dish of vegie lasagna and curry tofu with a quick bible study on the side.

She accommodated her mother because for the first time she had a glimpse of the driving force behind their disagreements and arguments. She resented her for a long time but today, she silently allowed her mother to dictate to her, her expectations. The conversation was never ending. Taniqua had to lie to her to get her to go home. She had had enough of church and religion.

"I am church out", she thought to herself.

"Sorry you have to go help your sick friend Ingrid. I was just getting into the nitty-gritty of the gospel".

"I promise you that I will call you if I have any questions".

"And don't let the children rip up the Bible. This is the fourth one I brought here".

"I will".

"Come by tomorrow".

"I really have to wash up and go see Ingrid", she insisted.

"Ok. Later then".

"Bye"

"Bye. I love you".

"I know. And Jesus loves me more".

"Isn't that the truth".

One Caucasian Boy

Flower Among Ash

It was another Indian summer day in the Fall and the community was bursting with life. People were out running errand while others were enjoying the day. Ketrel and Ingrid dropped off Taniqua at the apartment when they saw Duquan waiting in the parkette at the front of the apartment. They parked into the visitor's parking where they say him and joined him on the bench facing the sandbox. Taniqua didn't have much to say. It was awkward standing there and not having anything to say to him. They had not spoken since he left Taniqua and the children. The tension was broken when a U-Haul van pulled up. A Caucasian male came out and walked over to them.

"What's up guys? Can you tell me which entrance is closer to the elevator?

"You are kidding me, have you not seen the neighbourhood? What a white boy like you doing here, all the way to nowhere land?", Ingrid questioned him in amazement. "People like your kind live in Forest Hill. You on drugs or something?"

"I lived in Rosedale and now this place will be my home, you have a problem with that ma'am?"

"You didn't just call me ma'am? Do I look like a ma 'am to you? I am in my twenties!"

"I apologize. Can someone please tell me which is the closer entrance to the elevator, thanks"

"Why are you telling us thanks when we have not told you anything" Ketrel asked foolishly.

"In advance, I thank you", he clarified.

Duquan added his two cents, "The elevator is wherever you are; it can take you up and it can take you down"

"That does not answer my question"

"Does this place look like it holds an elevator? D, is there an elevator in this building? Taniqua you know of any elevator in this apartment? If there is one, it is not working. Why don't you use the stairs and get some exercise to build your scrawny muscles?", Ketrel teased him.

"Thanks for nothing. The building is more than ten stories tall, elevator service is manditory", he replied with annoyance and walked back to the van and drove to the back of the building.

"There goes the neighbourhood"

"That was rude Duquan" Ingrid scolded him.

"You were worst", he reminded her.

"I was making small talk"

"Yeah right" the others said in unison.

Ketrel query Duquan's comment, "What did you mean by there goes the neighbourhood? When a Caucasian family move into a community the real estate usually goes up and so does the property value but if a brother moves in, then that is when you say there goes the neighbourhood"

"That is what they have you to believe. Who do you think are the drug dealers? When we get caught, we make the six o'clock news but them, they bribe somebody and it's all a hush-hush as if it had never happened"

"Is that a testimony? Your new love is into them things?"

"That is none of your business"

"You're the one confessing Duquan"

"I'm just saying; whether up or down, they move in and things change"

"It's because we settle for mediocre why things remain the same", Taniqua finally speak. Who knows he might hold the MPP accountable for the weeks old garbage behind the building and then they will get fed up and do something about it"

"I want to know why we cannot make changes in our community" Ingrid asked.

"Who is going to listen to us. When you call your councillor's office, they want your name and the reason for the call, take your number and never get back to you. And we have names that say we are the typical black people except for Ingrid. But face it, what kind of names are those. Our parents sure did not make it easy for us. You think the MPP is going to return the call of Mr. Ketrel?"

"Mr. Ketrel", Ingrid laughed

"I have to big up myself. Here comes your new Caucasian tenant. How do you like the place so far" Ketrel called out.

He walked over, "Not what I had expected. It's a fixer upper. It will do. What can I expect for such a cheap rent?

"You thing the rent is cheap?" Taniqua asked feeling insulted.

"It's a bargain. It's a giveaway. Anyone can afford to live here"

"Then why don't you just give it away to some homeless person and go back to where you come from", Taniqua replied angrily. "What! You think this is some soap opera or sitcom and you are the token white boy that popped up for better ratings.

"You're confusing me"

"You are already confused. Coming here as if everyone can afford the rent, so what is it you want to say about us, yes, people who are sometimes late with the rent? Welfare recipient!"

"I am surely not getting off on the right foot with you guys. You lost me. You're not making any sense to me"

"I don't know what idea you have in your head from your Rosedale house but when you're here, you better get off your high horse. And another thing, you're not one of us"

"Just trying to blend in"

"Consider a mirror; you are white. You cannot blend in. Where this dude comes from? This is real for us"

"And your point is?"

"What is the true reason for you coming here to live? Trying to find yourself"

"If you must know, I've been doing everything my parent told me to, completed three years of university, got tired of the pampered life and here I am"

They all laughed.

"Tired of the pampered life", Duquan replied with amusement.

"The last time I check; this was a free country"

"So you're going to be that one Caucasian man in the grand scheme of things. It is like watching a network show with all black people and suddenly, here comes the white man, like that show, Girlfriends and she had to marry that short white guy and he stayed on for a couple of seasons. They tried it on Friends and the black girl Ross and Joey had a thing for, what happened? She got the boot. And you know why? They don't want to see black and white intimacy on TV so if you think you are this ideal white man in our story, whatever!" Taniqua was livid and lost her trail of thought.

"At least you did not call me a boy"

Ketrel interrupted, "What if we were all characters in a book and the writer chose to insert a white person in the equation to see how we would react. If we are prejudice or racist"

"The writer would already know that" Taniqua answered. Writers are like God; they know everything before it happens".

"For real, think about this; what if this white person… Ketrel said thinking aloud."

"This white person is still standing in earshot of this conversation", Tommy said playing along with the scenario,

"What if the writer is white?

"Only a white person would write a book that make black men look bad. If the writer is black, he or she would have the Black characters live in Rosedale with blue collar jobs", Ketrel continues.

"Be realistic. Nothing happened so far that is not real. I think if it is not God who predestined things to be this way and there is a writer, he or she is black and have lived in the ghetto" Ingrid tried to rationalized.

"Or, the writer is white with one black friend that lives in the ghetto and he or she is putting a spin on the experience and trying to write the opposite in the book and that is why I am here. I am the Caucasian male that has come to put a twist in the plot, maybe I will marry a black girl or save the community".

"You're just full of it. For a university student, you are dumb. Writer my foot" Taniqua added.

"Hey! I was just going with the flow".

"What if there are beings on other planets watching us like how we watch TV and laughing at us. This would be a drama or could be a Black soap opera with the one white man so they can see how we interact"

"Now you're getting creepy Ketrel. Let's go home. Duquan keep in touch, don't be a stranger. Taniqua see you later" She turned to her to the new tenant and asked, "By the way; what is your name?"

"Tommy"

"Typical" she replied. As she walked away she confided in Ketrel, "See, even white people have white names. Which BLACK boy you know name Tommy?

God, the Business Man

Taniqua decided to visit church for inspiration or direction as she continued her journey of self-fulfillment. Her faith in herself was dwindling with the thought of being the sole provider for herself and her children with the government student loan that she was getting.

Self-doubt and evidence of her past were far too much for her to be self-confident. She drew on the memory of the sermons she heard about God as El Shaddai in the past. Not trusting herself, she believed that church was the place she needed to be for the direction she needs to take. It was another fork in the road for her.

All these years of avoiding her mother's invitations, she finds herself yearning for what she had been trying to get away from. She had to cross that line risking encouraging her mother in her mission of taking up the yoke of Christ and follow him. She had outgrown the church and all the restriction. Her freedom caused nothing but pain. And now she must take the bull by the horn and face her fear. Her mother's lectures.

Hanging out with friends she had not seen a long time ago erased her anxiety. Her implicit knowledge of the Bible came back to memory with very little effort. "Pathfinder really paid of", she thought to herself. No one bagger her about her lifestyle. It was a judgement free zone. She felt safe enough to share in the discussion.

It was first Sabbath. Prayer and fasting. Taniqua lingered back with the small group for the service. They sang all her favorites even songs from earlier years. It was a celebration than the gloomy fasting she thought it would be. The group had just returned from feeding the homeless downtown Toronto and visiting the shut-in members that have not been to church in a while. "How did I not see this? She questioned herself. The new pastor was doing it the biblical way.

Her mother kept her distance which allowed her time to enjoyed her space and get answers to her questions. But it was more of a worship and fellowship experience with her long-lost friends and enjoying the senior members who were so eager to pray with her.

Testimony time came. She wanted to go to the front and share with the group her situation and request their prayers for her to help her make the right choice. As she thought about it, she realized that they all know that she had left the church. She went from a feeling of comradery to intimidation.

While she was debating with herself, Carol went up to the podium to share her testimony. Carol and Taniqua had been best friend all through Pathfinder. Their lives began to change when they get involved with friends that mocked them about the restrictions of their belief. They wanted to hang out with the popular girls. High school was their defying moment of choosing instant happiest their way. The pull was intoxicating for her to resist. Life was enjoyable. She sat there and wondered what was different between her and Carol. She looked at peace. Taniqua was in awe of Carol's demeanor and was drawn to what she was about to say.

"Amen church", she started.

"Amen", the church responded.

"Well, most of you know my life story so I will not be going into much details. What I can say to you is that I am a dreamer. I've dreamt of a better life than my mother had. I've watched her struggled to feed us and trying to keep a roof over our heads. I guess I focused so much on that until

Flower Among Ash

I became a statistic by becoming a teen mom, the very thing I was trying to avoid. It became my mantra. It was not long after that I changed that and start believing in myself again. I saw that all the celebrated people were writing books about their lives so I wrote a book of my own and praise God, I was favored. My children's book is now a best seller of the New York Times. To thank God for his goodness, I want to invest in the new church that we are building. I could have invested in any other company but I think God's work is a sure investment. I was also able to purchase a house and a car for cash. God can turn your life around that even you yourself will not believe it. It has been six years but God has been good to me and my girls. I'm sorry to be babbling but the Holy Spirit is very chatty today. I am just impress to share my story to you so you know that if any of you is in the situation that I once found myself, there is hope for you. God cares about your every need. He cares about all aspect of your life, even your business. I promised God that if He blesses me I would return His tithe and offering and invest in His work so that others can find hope in these times like I found hope in Him. If you do not get anything form my testimony, understand this, God cares and He will give you the desires of your heart if you abide in Him. God bless you all. Thanks for listening.

For a moment Taniqua was swallowed up in hope that she too could turn her life around but it was for a price. A price that she thought she was not ready to make. Does this meant that she should take the bull by the horn, strike while the iron is hot and just trust that God will never let her fall? That was an arduous task because she has been trusting herself all these years. Although it hadn't worked out for her but this was the extreme. Only if Duquan would marry her; her troubles would be over.

Taniqua's first step was to stand before the church and asked them to pray for her. She was then the core of a prayer circle that included her mother. They prayed until her knees cried out for mercy.

Taniqua turned to her mother at the end of service thinking that she was going to give her another lecture but instead her mother invited her to have lunch with her and the other members in the dining hall. She and Carol had a fun time reminiscing on their past as a teenager, camping, and competing with other clubs. It has been way too long that Taniqua had enjoyed a Sabbath with her friends and especially the good food.

Extended Church

Flower Among Ash

Taniqua stopped by Ingrid and Ketrel's apartment before going up to hers. They watched a movie while having popcorn and Seven-Eleven slushies. Duquan came in immediately after her.

She went over to open the curtain. "It is a beautiful day and outside is splendid. Who sits at home and watch movies in a make shift dark room and let such a perfect day go to waste?

"Have you never been to the movies in broad daylight before? It is the same thing", Ketrel informed her.

"What has gotten into you being all chirpy and all? Ingrid questioned.

"She met Jesus. That is the way church people get all doll up for Jesus, I thought he was dead", Duquan mocked her. "Nothing more than she is looking for one of them preacher man to step on my turf but I am not going to have none of that you hear me", he ridiculed her.

"You do not have any claim on me Duquan! People go to church for many different reasons. I invited all of you, my so-called friends to come with me and conveniently none of you were available".

"Why you all up into this church business? God knows where you live. I am not into all that to talk to God business. Church people say God is everywhere. Going to church make no sense. I am sure God is here enjoying the movie until you walked in here trying to make us feel bad. I can't hang with you anymore. It's like you are mutating in front of our very eyes to the point of being unrecognizable", Ingrid added.

"It wouldn't have kill you guys to come today. You

never want to do what I want to do. I just want to change up things a bit. What's wrong with that?

"Only money people go to church. They are always asking you for money and the more you give the more they want. That is not for me. I am broke", Ketrel said while emptying out his pocket.

"If you only know what I know. Apparently, God is giving back money to His followers. You remember Carol? She is a millionaire now".

"Say what? Ketrel interjected. "So when they say the Lord giveth and He taketh away, it that for real?

"For real. God gave her enough to buy a house and car with cash and still have enough to give the church one million dollars to build another church".

"That is what they do to get you coming. It is the church that give her the money so she can brag and then get other people to join. It is like the fake healing church. Do you know how many of those scams were found out? Duquan asked her.

"No'.

"Exactly! It is a set up".

"Why do you have to be so cynical Duquan?

"I believe you Duquan. Rich people don't go to church. They have more than enough so they don't need God for anything" Ketrel added.

"Tyler Perry is rich and he is a believer. TD Jakes and Joel Osteen has a lot of money and they go to church".

"Exactly! They have a lot of money because they are always begging poor people money and tell them that God says so", Duquan replied.

"God did say so".

Flower Among Ash

"How do you know that Taniqua?

"I read it in the Bible".

"The Bible was written by men", Ingrid jumped in the conversation.

"Whatever! I know Carol and she is rich and she said it is God she prayed to for help. There is nothing wrong with having hope of a better life than this. Look at the walls how they are pealing and the stench coming up from the garbage. Almost every summer the garbage collectors go on strike and leave us to live in our own waste. Is it so bad to want more? I shouldn't be surprised of the way you are all talking. If it is not God that is going to take us out of here, who will. We need a miracle to leave this dump. None of us are heirs to riches or trust-fund children. Our parents have nothing just like us. This is the last time I will ever invite you guys to church. It your lost", she yelled.

"What I would like to know is why you are insulting me to my face. My apartment might be dilapidated, yes, I know big words too, but you have no business talking like you don't live in this run-down community too. One day with God and you think you are better than us", Ingrid fumed.

"I will see myself out. It is like talking to the walls".

"Yes, you do that", Ingrid told her and slam the door behind her.

Sticking Around

Flower Among Ash

Taniqua was playing in the sandbox with her children when Tommy joined her. "They say once a man twice a child", he said as he approached her.

She turned around to see who it was, "When you have children, you do anything, almost anything to make them happy", she replied

"They are all yours?

"Oh gee! I am liking you even the more"

"Sorry if I offended you"

"Oh really. You need some home training on how to be tactful. You lack the wisdom on the people skill area"

"This you know from the one question I asked?

"Yes. I do not need to hear anymore, and yes, they are all my children and I am not ashamed"

"What is your name? Tanisha interrupted the two.

"What is your name? Tommy replied with a question

"You cannot answer a question with another question" Taniqua corrected Tommy

"My name is Tommy", he told Tanisha.

"I know what letter your name starts with", she said proudly.

"What letter is that? Tommy asked.

"Your name starts with the letter T. I am going to be six soon and I am going to graduate and I will be going to the first grade the next school year"

"When will that be?

"I don't know", she said shrugging her shoulders. "You should ask my mom. She is the one that told me all that stuff", she said and continued playing in the sand box.

"I bet you cannot tell me what letter my name ends

with? Tommy asked Tanisha to see how Taniqua would react.

"The last letter of your name is E. Tom…..meee. Isn't that right mommy? She replied with her focus on what she was building in the sand.

"Is she right mommy? Tommy teased.

"Leave my daughter alone. She is learning phonemes, which she is good at, and by the way, if you listen to the end sound of your name; it does sounds like an E. It is hard to distinguish the sound the letter Y makes at her age. Bug off!

Tanisha got back into the conversation," Mommy, is it a long or a short sounding O in Tommy? She asked.

"Lets ask Tommy". She turned her attention to Tommy, "Well, Tommy; is it long or short O?

"Short, I think" he replied feeling unsure.

"I think so too. It sounded like a short vowel", she answered and ran off to the swing.

"Are you here to push my buttons or it is hard for you to think that gifted children can live in the ghetto?

"Well, I've never met people living in places like this before"

"Why do you come here to live? Your view of the people living here is so dismal and minimal. Are you not afraid of getting too close to our grimes? Nevertheless, we are just disfranchised" Taniqua informed him.

He sat beside her in the sandbox, "It has been along time since I've been in a sandbox. Which University you attended?

"Life"

"Did you ever….

"High school"

"You speak as if you know a thing or two"

"Pardon moi. I speak like I know something. Were you expecting me to be illiterate? I am currently attending life's university. It gives you a higher degree than book knowledge. Book knowledge is not all that it is cracked up to be"

"Did you dropout of school?"

"You are so tactful and for your information, I almost graduated from high school. I could have. I was completing extra courses hoping to get a scholarship. I could if I wanted to but, I wanted more than just graduating with the minimal requirement plus I am currently in college"

"I like you"

"Once again, you are very tactful"

"So"

"You don't even know me. We met just a few weeks ago! How can you like me? OH! I see. You are here to fulfill some fantasy that you should be with a Black woman. After you've fulfill your mission, what then?

"Whatever you want"

"I get it. You see me with four children and you assumed that I am easy. I do not fall easy like the autumn leaves"

"Not from my perspective"

She stood up and was going to let him have a piece of her mind, "You are pitiful. You disgust me. From the moment I saw you; I knew I was not going to like you. Please leave me alone!

"Hey! I am just pulling your strings. By the way, you people claim that you are misplaced, misjudged or whatever, but it is ok for you to assume that I am not a nice guy. I could be the one for you. Your deliverer!"

"Why are you picking on me and my children? Is your

life so unfulfilling that you decided to take it out on me? I do not need to be delivered. I am quite happy. Do not feel sorry for me"

"Ok! Just trying to make conversation. I am a bit shy so I might say stupid things"

"Really!

"Lets start over. I see you are sensitive when it comes to certain subjects so I will not talk about that stuff. Ok, starting over; Nice day eh?

"I do not like you"

"I cannot blame you. What is your name?

"Taniqua, and you better not".

"I will leave that alone"

"No! Go ahead! Say what you want about my name. I know what you are going to say; I've heard it all"

"I decline"

"There is hope for you. At least you are teachable"

"There is hope for me"

"I guess"

"We can go out sometimes; you said there is hope for me"

"I was referring to, never mind; I have a man"

"So"

"You are lame Tommy"

"Don't knock it until you try it"

"I cannot believe my ears. You are unbelievable", she told him and got up from out of the sandbox and dust off her jeans. "I will not dignify that with a reply; furthermore, you could be a sandbox killer. You people commit the most unthinkable crime. Leave, or I'll call the police," she warned him.

Flower Among Ash

"The police come in this neck of the woods? he jeered her. "I just like the way you look in those tight-fitting jeans"

"I was sitting in the sandbox having a peaceful time with my children and you have to come to disturb it".

"I apologize. Do you believe in love at first sight? From the moment I saw you, I thought, I must have that girl"

"And the girl does have a mind of her own. Tommy, do you know that I am BLACK?

"And my knees are weak. I never felt like this for people like you, your type"

"How romantic", she replied feeling insulted. People like me; BLACK people. Is that the way you court a woman to show interest in you? Those lines are sick and sick in the worst way"

"What are you saying, you could never see yourself with a white guy?

"I see myself in the future with a career and living a middle-class life that God blessed me with; not by sleeping around, heavens know I have been down that path and see where it got me"

"Are you giving up on men in general because of one bad experience or it is just white men you do not like"

"I've never been with a Caucasian man before"

"Not too late to try. A little milk for your coffee"

She laughed, "Thanks for the humour but I do not drink coffee and I am also lactose intolerant. Tommy, you have a good day. I have better things to do with my time"

"We should do this more often. You will like me once we get to spend more time together"

"It is either you are a fool or hopeful but I am not staying to find out"

"I did enjoy my time with you. It was a rocky start but it will get better. I do like you Taniqua. Trust me! I will not hurt you"

"Said the spider to the fly" she replied as she got the children and left him standing in the sandbox alone.

He shouted after her, "See you tomorrow, same time. I will be waiting. We can write out names in the same. Look! I am writing; Tommy loves Taniqua"

Without looking behind her, she said, "You can stay there and play Jesus all by yourself. Write all you want in the sand. You have a good one Tommy?

Big Brother is Looking

Flower Among Ash

Taniqua immediately went to the convenient store across the street to get milk for her children. She was eye shopping when Duquan walked over to her. "What are you trying to prove? he asked her.

"Duquan, I am not a mind reader. You have to give me more to go with," she answered looking a bit confused.

"I see you got the fever too. Isn't that hypocrisy?

"I am clueless to what you are talking about"

"Don't pretend with me. I see with my own two eyes that you got the jungle fever"

"TOMMY? You are delirious!

"What was going on in the sandbox?

"None of your business"

"You are my business"

"When was that? I did not get that memo Duquan"

"I am making it my business"

"You like to play in the fowl coop but I cannot?

"You and my children are all that matter to me and I am not going to sit by while some guy move in on my turf".

"Some white guy. Is that what you meant Duquan? Why can I not be with a white man?

"You are my family!"

"Said the visiting parent. We are all the family you have. Let me tell you something Duquan. If I want to have jungle fever, pneumonia, or the flu, it is my business, not yours. Stop watching me. You want to control me while you have every woman on the block plus your milk duds. I am an adult. I need no supervision. What Tommy and I did in the sandbox is none of your business"

"Were you touching each other?

"OK, do this one thing for me, pay for this milk". She

got distracted with what her daughter was doing. "Tanisha, put that back. I told you repeatedly, NO" she reprimanded her daughter who had taken up a pack of donuts.

"But mommy! Please! Please!", Tanisha pleaded.

"Let her have the donut" Duquan insisted.

"Because you are always around for them and there when they get hyper on sugar to keep them occupied. I said no"

"She is my daughter"

"Thanks for reminding me. I had forgotten that you are her father. It seems that they are your children when you are bored".

"How did you two made the arrangement? He just moved in like a few weeks ago"

She replied coyly, "I think I remembered seeing him moving in and he walked over to us; you know the rest"

"You exchange phone numbers in the elevator; the lobby? You want me to walk you home should he want to get friendly?

"Save me from the big bad white guy name Tommy. My gosh! His name is Tommy for crying out loud! I am at the age of consent; to do as I want with whomsoever I want without interrogation from you or anyone".

"What have you consented to? Is he coming over later? I was planning to spend the night or we can go out and see a movie. It has been a long while since we went out on a date. What do you think?

"I'll pass"

He turned to Tanisha for help. "Tanisha, want to go to the movie later and we could get some burgers after"

Flower Among Ash

"That is so low. She is just a pawn to your scheme. So, we go to the movie, then what?

Tanisha rushed to his side and hugged him. "Are you being honest daddy?

"Honest"

"We are going to have fun together, right mommy? And daddy, and Raven, and Rae and DJ, we are all going to have fun as one big happy family.

See how exciting she is; do you want to disappoint her?

"One big happy family. Who are you, Medea? what a joke! I guess we are going to the movie"

"We cool? He took the items from her hands, "Let me go and pay for these then we go home and find out what's playing at the movie. You should be careful these days. With all the crimes happening in the city and all. Tommy seems like an honest guy but you don't know these days. You are my family and I am not going to let anyone hurt you"

"What part do I play in this drama in your head?

"Are you planning to dump me for him?

"Lets go Duquan. Keep your nose out of my affairs"

Not a Fan

Flower Among Ash

Not one was prepare for what was to come this day during worship. It is true that the church is a hospital for people seeking spiritual healing among other needs. You would have to be flexible and tolerable to be a member of a church. The dynamic of believers creates its own soap opera.

Church goers are no different from other families. Especial single mothers who dreamed of their daughter marrying into a reputable family; a family that holds key role in the ministry of the church. Clara was one of them. She had her eyes on a suited mate for her daughter. What happened that day at church; the drama ministry couldn't duplicate. The floodgate that was about to be unleash on the congregation was from a silent storm that had been brewing for the longest time. The straw that broke the camel's back happened during choir practice the night before.

Apparently, Quinisha and the associate pastor's son were dating for quite sometime. They were so in love that they chose the same university to attend far away from home so that their relationship could grow away from the scrutiny of their parents and nosy members who took it on themselves with the notion of leading them in the right path.

Sister Clara was a busy body in church. She volunteers herself for every ministry the associate pastor would thought of just to impress him and to demonstrate her loyalty to the mission. She got clingier when she got whiff that the pastor was told that Quinisha was not a good fit for his son. That news dove her into a cooking frenzy for the pastor and his family and claimed that her daughter made the meal. She was desperate.

The tension was eased when the two finally moved away for school. She found herself back to square one that

Friday night at choir practice when she saw another member introducing her daughter to the pastor's son and watching them sitting there for a long time enjoying each others company.

Sister Clara had her instabilities in her past relationships. She was married four times. Her last husband died in a car crash that she was driving. She walked away unscaled. They were arguing because of jealousy. She thought that he was a no good of a man like her other husbands. She never trusted him. Now she spends her life making sure that Quinisha finds a suitable husband.

She was watching her dream crumble before her eyes. It confirmed the rumors. Quinisha told her that all was going well in the relationship but her youthfulness didn't afford her the wisdom to see beyond the physical. Clara was not too far off with her assumption. Her first two husbands were infidels. They had families outside the marital home. The third husband just left her without any explanation. Her insecurities and doting behaviours choke the relationship.

Sister Clara walked up to the pulpit just before the senior Pastor began to preach. She was fearless. "Good afternoon saints" she said calmly and with poise. "I know most of you have heard of what happened last night and some of you might or might not be surprised but here is where a lot of you will be blown away. I am not here to apologize. I have no regret of how I reacted. I was pushed beyond my limit and that is so much I can take. So, I am not a role model anymore, I gave in to my carnal mind and hit my brother".

The Pastor tried to intervene but she insisted. "Please let me speak my mind sir", she said to him. She continued to address the congregation. "I know the next thing that will

Flower Among Ash

happen is for the church to revoke my membership. If my membership was this piece of paper", she took up a sheet of paper from the Pastor's sermon and ripped it into small pieces, "This is what I would do with it. Why am I being attack by my family; my church family. My husband is gone and it seems it is open season to attack my family and me. I am trying hard with my daughter to stay in the faith and to marry a young many that will bring glory to God. It was her father's dying wish. Now she is home broken hearted and embarrassed and wants nothing to do with God. You see, this attack is not just physically but spiritual. All Quinisha did was to have a crush on a boy. They were dating. They planned to go away to the same university. She is so in love with him. Every time we facetime or text each other she would tell me about life was good with them not knowing that people were pushing another woman on him. She is so heart broken and ashamed to be so foolish not to see this coming. I warned her but she thought I was making up stuff because of my bad experience. Now she wants nothing to do with the church, God, and the school.

The pastor tried to regain the pulpit.

"Please let me speak," she continued. "Please give my daughter a fighting chance for a good relationship".

The pastor motioned to the sound crew to turn the mic off and explained to her that speaking to the congregation in such manner on such a private topic inappropriate. To get the congregation back in the mind of worship, they sang a few songs and prayed for the young people that God would to steer them in the direction that He wants them.

The young man in question joined Clara in the prayer room to explained to her that he had broken up with Quinisha weeks ago but she has been in denial. He apologized for not letting her know about their non-existing relationship. It was like rubbing salt in a raw wound. Even though it has it quick healing elements, it still hurts.

Later that day after the sermon she apologized to the congregation for her brawl both times. The deaconesses ran to her side like bees to a hive to comfort her and to pray with her.

Taniqua seeing all this thought of her mother and how she wanted the best for her. She saw her mom in Clara the pain that her decision has cost her. Taniqua was lost in her thoughts when her mother came and sat beside her.

"Not now *mother*", she said emphasizing on the word mother.

"I wont lecture you. I just want to know that all my craziness is because I love you and wants the best for you", she explained.

"Isn't that lecturing?

"No. It is me telling you that I might not like the way you are living but you're still me daughter. I love you", she told her and walked away.

It was a strange moment for Taniqua. Even trying to say I love you to her mother was challenging. "What have I become? She questioned herself. She remembered when her mother was her world but now they were worlds apart.

Let's Talk Over Lunch

Flower Among Ash

Taniqua had Sabbath lunch at Ingrid's apartment. It has been a very long time since the two went to church together. Ketrel made curry chicken with mash potato and carrot and white rice with the anticipation of guests coming over. They sat down to lunch when Ingrid brought up what happened at church relating to Sister Clara. Taniqua hinted on not repeating what happened at church before the guys but her disapproval was ignored. Ingrid gave Ketrel and Duquan blow-by-blow descriptions of what had happened at church. Not a word was misplaced. It was as if she was a human recorder.

Duquan eyes were fixed on Taniqua for most of the replay. He finally spoke to her, "Church was hot today. How comes you are so silent? Are you too ashamed of your perfect little church crumbling?

"The church is not crumbling. It is founded on Christ the rock!"

"Rock of ages clef for me. Can you not think for yourself?

"It is just one big misunderstanding. We are all people with weaknesses. No one said believers were perfect people. Unbelievers are the ones who are putting us on a pedestal and when something happen they use it as a reason not to join the church"

"They, like me?

"If the cap fit Duquan. Why am I on trial?

"Because you act so….

"I want to live per God's principle. Is there anything wrong with that? Ketrel back me up"

"Ketrel you keep out of this. Look at you! Four children

and you are not married and still you act as if you are holier than thou. Like you are not a sinner like any of us".

Taniqua was shocked hearing the words coming out of Duquan' mouth. She kept on eating with her eyes into her plate. "Is that what all of you think of me? She looked up at her friends. "I have sinned. I am an unwed mother. I want to live for Christ and I want to get married but you do not want to marry me Duquan" The tears rolled down her cheeks. "I want us to be a family in Gods eyes. I love you but all I am to you is your mattress. Sister Clara has her pain and disappointment too. We are humans. Believers are humans who sometime have sinned. God is not through with us. I am just another person in the dumps with high hopes and big dreams. Is that so wrong? While I have the breath of life in me, God can fix my brokenness Duquan. Tell me Duquan, what do you have against God? Why don't you give your life to God and show us sinners how it is done? Stop pointing your finger at me" she got up and threw the napkin into her unfinished meal. "I am tired of you not respecting me. I am not going to wait for you to come around and marry me. I regret the day we met. I regret sleeping with you. I regret being in love with you. Our relationship has been nothing but a pain to our children and me. You are the biggest mistake I have ever made. If singleness is my plight, so be it". She looked at Ingrid in dismay, "Have you ever walked a mile in Sister Clara or Quinisha shoe before you condemned her or me? She spoke out from her pain. "I will be enrolling in Bible classes. I would advice that you do too and then you'll be more informed on religion. You can join me or continue doing what we call life"

Ingrid did not take her rebuke kindly. "I live my life as I

please. Don't blame me for you not being able to keep your man. I know how to satisfy my man and that is why he does not cheat on me"

"Is that how you feel too Ketrel?

"*DO NOT* get me into this" Ketrel spoke up. "I do not need God to tell me how to be a father to my children and to be faithful to my woman. I am not a regular church goer like you but I know a thing or two"

"Good for you Ketrel" Taniqua replied. "Thanks for the meal. I was not expecting an ambush as a side dish. I will take my children and leave. I am done, C'est fini"

"We are just talking. You Christian can take life so serious. Lightened up. Sit down. I will walk you home. DJ and Raven are still sleeping. Sit. Finish your meal. You cannot take life so serious" Duquan said without apologizing.

She looked at Ingrid's face and saw no remorse. "I am who I am. I am a child of God and it is about time I live like one. Therefore, I believe certain things should not be discussed among unbelievers so that it does not become a stumbling block to them and their salvation"

"You are having premarital sex like the rest of us Taniqua! You are not better than me" Ingrid lashed out at her. "This is my home and I can share whatever I feel like sharing about what happened at church without you preaching to me. You are judging me from your pedestal. Did not your *HOLY BIBLE* told you not to judge. I am not the one who made your life miserable, so leave. I am not stopping you"

"Tanisha, lets go"

"C'mon! Ingrid. That's taking it too far", Ketrel

interjected." Both of you have been friends forever. Let's change the subject. Duquan, get the Irish Moss.

"I am leaving Ketrel. Duquan, I've been through with you for a long time now. I will never take you to court to support our children. God has provided for the birds and clothe the grass, God Himself will take care of the fatherless and the lonely like myself. I pledge today between my soul and God to do right amid your neglect to be a father to your children. Michael will stand up for me….

"Who is this Michael" Duquan asked ignorantly.

"Jesus" Ingrid informed him.

"When did Jesus change His name to Michael? I thought God does not change. How cozy. You and JC are chump that He is now Michael" Duquan teased.

"You are so ignorant" Ingrid butted in. "Sit down Taniqua. Duquan is the one attacking you. Maybe your prayers are being answered that is why he is acting like a jerk"

"Is that so? Duquan asked Ingrid without taking his eyes off Taniqua.

"I could not eat another bite. I just want to be by myself. Later"

Taniqua was going towards the door when Ketrel asked for her to wait until he made her a plate for her to take home. He showed her the topper ware with the rice. "Is this enough? She continued walking towards the door. She addressed him without looking behind her. Take my fatherless children home for me please Ketrel. Thanks for lunch" she told him and closed the door behind her.

Bridging the Gap

Flower Among Ash

Taniqua was asleep when the children came home. Tanisha and Rae were asleep too. DJ got his bottle and went back to sleep. Raven was wide-awake and eating her dinner when Taniqua came out and saw Ingrid, Ketrel and Duquan.

"Have I not had enough of your chastisement that you have to come to unleashed your wrath upon me again?"

"No one said anything! We know that what happened earlier was not cool but you act all higher than thou most of the time", Duquan said trying to justify himself when Ketrel cut him off.

"Stop Duquan. I wanted to see, we wanted to see if you were ok", he corrected himself as he spoke on the behalf of the others. "I am sorry about what happened and I did not want the day to end with you feeling the way you did when you left the apartment. We have been a family ever since I can remember. We have been through a lot. I agree with what you are trying to say about the way you want to live your life. I try to tell D here to change his ways and be a better man. Do not turn your back on him, for your children sake"

"What other choice do I have? You see how miserable I am because of our living arrangement"

"Prayer works, right D", Ketrel added as he addressed Duquan

"I was not praying for nothing", he replied

"How could you be so dense? Ingrid added

"You want to gang up on me now? Duquan asked with hostility"

"No one is ganging up on you. You need to be responsible for your children. You have two sons and two daughters. You need to be a better example to them," Ketrel scolded him.

"Ketrel, God is my provider" Taniqua added. "I will be fine guys. I am the problem to this equation. Thanks again for dinner and the goodies you brought over but this is where I get off"

"Get off? What do you mean by that? Ingrid asked with an attitude that Taniqua was eluding to ending their relationship.

'Take it as you will", she replied and went to the cupboard for a can of apple juice.

Ketrel walked over to her and rest his hand across her shoulders, "I appreciate you helping me to be where I am in getting a skill and even a trade soon. What I am saying is you have changed my life and my family. I am earning more money and I do not have to stress myself with temporary agency work to find me a job. Tell me, when you said this is where you get off, you're just talking Duquan, right", he asked in dismay. You are a part of my family. You've changed my life. Don't cut us all off because of Duquan, you need our help. I will stand by you. Think about how our children get along with each other and we are alternate godparents and babysitters. We have a thing going right now that is good and you two are suppose to be soul mates".

"Excuse me! I am leaving and I will talk to you later", Ingrid said resenting Ketrel getting involve "You can join her crusade but remember whom you are sleeping with tonight", she continued and left slamming the door violently behind her.

He turned towards Duquan but he spoke before Ketrel could say a word, "I am out. Your woman is different".

"Different how?

"You know. Not like her"

Taniqua interjected, "Thanks again Ketrel but if you want to talk to him, please do it outside". She walked to the door and open it, "He does not live here and I would prefer you not taking your friends over without asking for my consent. We will keep in touch".

"You are so full of it!", Duquan told her as he passed her at the door. Ketrel hugged her and left behind Duquan.

Youth Opportunity Explosion

After the incident with Clara, you would think the leaders of the church would be more sceptical of whom they lent the pulpit to, but today was going to be another earth-shaking day.

The church is lenient with giving the youth in the church the opportunity to be a part of the ministry. One of their belief is: God gave talents and gifts to be used and the church is where they should be nurtured and developed by using them to spread the gospel of Jesus Christ.

With that in mind; Nicholas Gary, age twenty-five had the privilege to present the Word of God to the congregation. He started out with the traditional introduction about himself, a snip-bit story and prayer.

What most people did not know that prior to coming to Canada, Nicholas lived in seven different foster homes in his lifetime. He had been through a great ordeal. After the fact, some members complained to the pastoral staff that they failed to screen those who would use the pulpit. They were concern about the church's reputation and demanded that the pastoral staffs were to screen everyone by reviewing and editing their sermon prior to speaking. But Nicholas was not talking verbatim from his script. He spoke from his heart, his experience.

Whether it was lack of monitoring, a direct intent or the Holy Spirit's leading, his cup runneth over. Nicholas had some ups and downs in his relationship with God. He has been mentored by the first elder and seems to be doing better after the questionable relationships.

The tears welled up at his throat as he began to speak. "God will provide a way of escape for those that need it", he spoke timely. "He will not give you more than you can bear but what about me? I have had many mothers and fathers but where was God to give me a way of escape? I know it is said that all things work for a good to them that love God and are called per his purpose. I have been waiting to uncover the purpose of my abuse of my past. I am trying to be the best that I can be but it is hard", he sobbed. "I married my wife because of my twin daughters so that they would have some stability. I am hurting on the inside under this facade".

Looking out into the congregation on his biological mother who had given him up because she was a teen mother and her parents were too poor to provide for another child or grand-child.

"I begged God for your mama. I wanted you to come and save me. I looked for you. You did grow up. You could have come for me but instead you went on and start a new family without me. Why me mama? How comes you kept all the other children but me mama? What did I ever do to you that you could not take the time to make sure a decent couple adopted me mama? Was that too much for you to do? You kept everyone else but me. You breast fed them, change their diapers, celebrated their birthdays and for me; you gave me up to delinquents. I thought I was over it but seeing you again brought it all back to me. I chose God but who chose me? I am tired of looking for love and to be important enough for someone to fight for".

The pastor and the elder joined him and wrapped their arms around him. The pastor spoke addressing him and the congregation. "I tell you Nicholas that God truly cares for you. He died for you. If you were the only one earth, he would have died for you nevertheless. Congregation, people

Flower Among Ash

are hurting, like Nicholas, please consult with any of the pastors or any members of the prayer ministry when you seem burden with the perplexities of life. We are here for you. Let us support each other. The prayer ministry team please meet me in my office immediately. Remember that next weekend is our prayer vigil for our youths and you can see why we need to pray for them. Please support our youths. I apologize for stopping the sermon abruptly but little Sophia will bring us the second sermon". As he spoke, the elder escorted Nicholas to the pastor's office.

Sophia walked up to the podium. The pastor introduced her to the congregation. "Sophia is twelve years old and an honor students at her school. She likes cats and her favorite sports is hokey. She is also an active Pathfinder and enjoys going downtown to feed the homeless. Her mother told me that she saves her allowance to buy food for those in need. She doesn't stop there; she has adopted two of her friends at school to share here lunch with them when they have nothing to eat. Most importantly, she loves Jesus and is allowing herself to be let by His spirit in helping others. Sophia, the pulpit is yours", he concluded and headed to his office.

What the pastor did not tell the congregation was that Sophia had a great sense of humor. Within five minutes of the sermon, the congregation had forgotten Nicholas' melt down. It seems that there was always an overspill of emotions that unleashes on the unsuspecting congregation. The flip side of the coin was that the church seems to be the haven for people like Taniqua who felt that they are alone in their crucibles. And that was what Taniqua looking for; a place that is non-judgemental, a haven even with its surprising leaks of emotional outbursts.

Being ambivalent in her feeling and not having a clear answer to her question. At the risk of loosing her friends and the chance of marrying Duquan, Taniqua was contemplating on joining the church with all its Biblical requirements.

Her mother came over and invited her to lunch at the house. Taniqua gave in and went to appease her. Tanisha is always excited to spend time with her grandmother. She was even more thrilled about Sophia preaching and want to be like her someday.

"I want to be a preacher too like Sophia when I am twelve years old mama", she told her grand-mother.

"You can be whatever you want by God's choosing", she answered.

All the chatting couldn't erase the awkward silence between Taniqua and her mother.

"Thanks for the invitation mother".

"I remember when you usually called me mom".

"Please do not start. I have enough on my plate".

"I am going home. I will pick up the children later. Bye", she told her mother and close the door behind her.

"But you just got here", her mother said but Taniqua was long gone through the door. "These young people are so temperamental".

Hands off Training

Flower Among Ash

It was very difficult for Taniqua to stay angry with Ingrid for too long. She went by Ingrid's apartment to apologize to her. They were back to their old self again. The following Sabbath Ingrid took the subway with Taniqua to church instead of letting Ketrel take her.

Sabbath School had ended and they were singing a few hymns from the hymnal to transition into the next part of the service. The first song was "Bringing in the Sheaves" Ingrid and Taniqua joined in when she turned Ingrid's attention to her mother and Tanisha sitting at the opposite side of the church.

"Look at her! It finally came to me why my mom act so strange with Tanisha sometimes"

"What are you talking about? Ingrid asked and continues to sing, "We shall come rejoicing bringing in the sheaves" she paused, "Let go and let God", she continues to sing, bringing in the sheaves, bringing in the sheaves"

"I know she loves her but when she comes here, it is different. She is so concern about what the church people thinks about me getting pregnant in high school and having three children….

"Four", Ingrid corrected her.

"I though you were not listening me"

"I have two ears"

"Her face drooped when Tanisha came near her. While she was introducing her to her Deacon friends. She barely opens her mouth. It has been five years now……

"It takes some people longer to get over disappointment, but I think it is all in your head. Sing, it will make you feel better"

"No, it's not in my head. I can see it on her face and it

is only when we are at church. If you could see them at the apartment and in the mall.

"Now that you mention it. I think she does not like the fact that you are with Duquan?

"Nope. It is her lovely daughter. I guess she was not bargaining that coming to Canada would mean she had to give up her parenting rights. This hands-off parenting does not work with West Indian children".

"Why would you say something like that?

"We don't know how to handle all that sudden change from being in a dictatorship home where what she says goes and no question asked, you know what I mean. Do as I say and not as I do. Leaving that type of home life to a country where the roles are reverse. My gosh! You know how many times I threatened to call the police on her when I wanted to have my own way. And being the good Christian she is, she just let me have my way".

"And look at you now"

"Exactly!

"I am not affirming your theory. You must get past this guilt. So what! You got pregnant and the baby daddy that is not supporting you or the children in anyway, shape or form, but look at the bright side, you did almost graduate from high school and now you're back in school. God forgave you and I know your mom does"

"But it did not have to be that way"

"Why are you so hard on yourself?

"I deeply regret how I treated mom, trying to be Canadian and all eh!

They laughed

"But it was your past, you will have a brighter future

when you graduate, God is not done with you yet, isn't that what you told us last time"

"Why I had to take the long and difficult path?

"C'est la vie"

"Most of my pathfinder friends are in prestigious jobs with degree, honestly, it pains me probably more than mom how I messed up"

"Please get out of this funk, its Sabbath, Praise the Lord!".

"I guess. If I could do it all again" Taniqua sighed.

"I don't say I am proud of myself for dropping out of school but I am not going to beat up on myself. Life is too short for me to tie myself down in a classroom, with my nose in books all day and night like you. You don't go to parties anymore. School was not for me; this girl just wants to have fun and live in the present. God might even come before you graduate and then you would have wasted your time studying for nothing. It is like I said, C'est la vie"

"Sometimes you scare me when I hear stupidity coming from your lips"

"I might be stupid, miss soon to be certified dental assistance but are you happy? That is all I am saying".

"I could not settle with that"

"And the man you are pining away for"

"That was low Ingrid"

"You went there when you called me stupid"

"I did not mean that you are stupid, it's just"

"What are you going to do when you get your degree, dump me? Oh, I see! I am the stupid one now that you will have your degree and all. I guess you will be out of my league now.

"You know I'm not like that"

"That is what you say now. I guess you and your Ivy League, degree wearing friends who didn't care for you during the hard times will hook up"

"Wait up! you are dead wrong about me. The things that comes out of your mouth really scares me"

"I know, it is stupid. You are already morphing"

"I am sorry if I made you feel bad. I love you and sorry to dump my stuff on you like that"

"You have to respect me and my decision and don't try to make me feel bad for not wanting to go back to school. School is not for everyone"

"Got it! My apology"

"No problem. Now let us worship. My baby daddy is over there bragging everyday that he is studying to do Drive Clean. I am just sick of it. This is who I am, and I am content. God accepts me as I am so everybody else should live with it. People change. I know you will change too. You are ever being too busy to hang out with us these days".

"I want good grades. I am going to school on a loan and if I do not pass, where will I get the money to repay my student loan. C'mon. I am a single parent going to school without much help and besides that, I want to move out of the ghetto"

"Just like I said; People change".

"That is not fair. I work hard for this. I deserve this!

"I. I. I. The very thing that caused Lucifer to be kicked out of heaven".

"That is it; forget it. Forget I'd said anything to you"

"You talked my man into going back to school and ever since both of you have been going back to school, you are trying to recruit everyone else. Give it a rest" You got Ketrel, let it go!

"I guess I know how you truly feel now. I promise, I will never try to persuade you to get a higher education or any skills of such"

"I am not so educated but I know your kind"

"You're my friend. I only want what is best for you"

"And that is to go to school and get a skill"

"YES!"

"I have nothing else to say. I know what you think of me since, whatever; don't expect to see me at your graduation next week. Excuse me" she got up and went to sit two pews closer to the front.

Feeling more confused than ever, "What just happened here? I started out talking about my mom's embarrassment then out of now where, a slap in the face. Boy! I did not see this coming. What am I supposed to do now, Jesus? She is my best friend. I never meant to make her feel bad about herself. I wanted her to do well and I thought going back to school was the way to change our life. Isn't that what friends do?

The twins shook her back to reality. It was story-time. She gave them each a loony and started to sing the story-time song, "Red is the colour of my favourite rose, green is the colour of the grass" as she takes them up for the story time. Her eyes could not avoid Ingrid as she passed her. Ingrid took her children the opposite side of the alter and avoided making eye contact with Taniqua.

Staying Connected

Flower Among Ash

It rained all weekend. Taniqua had not seen Ingrid since last Saturday. They usually meet at Ingrid's apartment before leaving for church. Taniqua went to meet her. She knocked on the door a few times but no one answered. She could hear the children playing inside. She thought it did not matter to Ingrid that she could hear the children playing in the apartment. She assumed she was sending her a message that she is no longer interested in their friendship.

Tanisha called Lamisha, "Lamisha open the door!

Answering behind the door, "Hi Tanisha! Are you going to church?

"Open the door; my mom wants to come in".

"Hi auntie Taniqua! We are not going to church today. Can you tell my mom to let me come with you?

Tanisha banged on the door, "Open the door Misha! I must go peeee!

"My mom said I am not allowed. Can you ask my mom to let me come with you to church?

There was a sudden hush at both side of the door. Taniqua took Tanisha back to the apartment to use the bathroom then went to church with her children.

It was Sunday evening and Taniqua decided to break the silence. She called Ingrid and hang up at the first ring. She practiced what she was going to say to her, then called again. Her heart pounded with every ring then as she heard a voice, she hanged up the phone. She sighed, "This is stupid, she is my friend. Why am I so nervous? I did nothing wrong; I think" she thoughtfully picked up the phone and dialed the number again. The waiting was intense. The answering machine came on. The beep stopped for a few second when Taniqua realized that she had to start leaving her message.

"Hi! It's me. I guess you are not home. Aaammm, so, what's up, aaahh, it is still raining; those meteorologists do not know a thing about weather. Hold up! I have a beep, it must be you calling." She answered the other line but it was not Ingrid. Duquan was in the lobby with grocery. She hangs up the phone and went downstairs for the grocery. She had forgotten about the phone call until after dinner as she was looking for a plastic container to store some leftover in the refrigerator. She picked up a purple top clear plastic container that Ingrid had brought her some chicken foot soup in when she was ill a few weeks ago.

"Goodness" she said alarmingly as she remembered that she was making a call before Duquan showed up. She hurried to the phone; the machine came on, "Ingrid! I found your purple top container" she started out sounding enthusiastically. She paused and thought about what she wanted to say. She spoke sincerely, "Sorry for insulting you the other day. I did not intentionally mean to. You are right to say that I have changed. I have not only changed because of what I have learned at school but the way I see things. I have a different view of life now. The possibilities in life are better for me now. I did not mean to be a snob. I wanted to change with you and sorry for forcing my views on you. I will respect your way of life, it is just that I feel guilty about my life and how I've ruined it but all that will change, have changed. It is like they say at church; which was not the same without you, but it is said if something does not bother you that it is ok for you but if it is eating away at you then you should do something to fix it, and that is what I am doing. That is what I have done, so I guess we both should see things from each other perspective and just leave it at that. I

Flower Among Ash

am not saying I will not miss you at my graduation but my big day is Tanisha's birthday. Mom is planning to have a double celebratory party at her place. Mom is finally happy with me. She brought me pamphlet about going further with my education. She wants me to be a Dentist. Enough about me; so call my mom or me and let either of us know if you will be there. Pass the word to Ketrel and bring the children. Anyway, I want to stay connected with you. The longer we stay mad at each other; it is more likely that our friendship will dissolve. I don't know if you got my entire message; the beep might have gone off and I did not hear it. Anyways, later". She hanged up the phone feeling relieved.

"Somehow I do not see the wrong I did her", she said to herself. "I might become a Dentist; then what? She is going to malice me. Jesus, you know my heart; I just wanted to do right by my mom and myself. This must be a growing pain. It hurts;

Lord it is you and me again. We have some studying to do for my finals. I guess I am going through my Job experience".

TAG! You're It

Flower Among Ash

Tanisha was excited and looking forward to the big day she turns six. It was the day when Taniqua would be graduating and it was also Tanisha's birthday. They had a mother daughter day of shopping, hair and make-up for Taniqua. They came home and tried on different outfits before picking the perfect suit for their big day. Suddenly there was a knock on the door.

"Mama, it must be daddy", Tanisha said excitedly to her mother.

"How many times must I tell you that your grandmother is mama; I am mom" Taniqua replied.

Tanisha was not listening to her mother, "May I open the door mama?

"What did I just tell you?

"I hear the knock again"

"Go!

Tanisha went to open the door and came back into the bedroom, "It was Mr. Tommy"

"What did he want?

"I don't know"

"What did he say to you?

"He can answer that; mine if I come in. Although I am physically inside already", said Tommy as he walked towards the bedroom door.

Taniqua was shocked. "What are you doing here?

"Your daughter let me in", he replied

She turned towards Tanisha to discipline her, "Go to your room"

Tanisha went to the living area sulking and sat down on the day bed that she sleeps on. Taniqua came out into the living area and send Tanisha into the bedroom so she can talk with Tommy, "Go into the room!

"But you told me to go to my room"

"Go to my room"

She headed towards the bedroom again.

"I did not want to get you into trouble Tisha", Tommy tried to apologize.

"My name is Tanisha! Not Tisha", she corrected him and disappeared into the room.

"What do you want Tommy? I am not comfortable having you here like this", Taniqua reproved his presence.

"You can offer me a drink"

"I have no alcohol here"

"Why do you assume that I was talking alcohol?

"Please leave. As I've said, I do not feel comfortable with you in my home"

"May I have a glass of water?

"This is an apartment; we do not pay for our water. The water from your tap in your apartment is drinkable". She was about to push him out when Tanisha came out wearing one of her outfit.

"Look Mr. Tommy", she said proudly as she showed off her outfit. "I am wearing this to my birthday party"

"WOW! Today is your birthday?

"NO, Silly! Thursday is my birthday", she answered and ran back into the bedroom and came out again with an invitation. "This is for you Mr. Tommy. I want you to come to my party and mama will be graduating too".

"Mama? Who is Mama?

"My mother, you are silly goose"

Taniqua interjected, "Tanisha go back to the room; I

Flower Among Ash

will be there a bit. I want to speak to Mr. Tommy and then I will come to help you pick out an outfit".

Before Tanisha could leave the room, Tommy let himself out and leaned on the doorpost.

"Congrats! You did it. Good for you."

"Thanks".

"I guess I will see you at the party"

"It will be a children's party"

"But you will be celebrating your graduation too, so"

"You are sick. I know what you are doing. Why would you accept an invitation from a little girl?

"Why you did not tell her that you do not want me to go to her party?

"I did not want to break her heart".

"Why are you fighting this, us?

That was enough for Taniqua to slam the door in his face.

He shouted from the outside the door, "See you at the party mama!".

Milestone Reached

Flower Among Ash

Taniqua was very emotional on her big day. She and Tanisha were extremely elated that the day finally arrived. It meant that both will start a new chapter in their lives. Tanisha will start first grade while Taniqua will have a certificate to make it official that she is a dental assistance.

The boys were still asleep and the two had an intimate breakfast together. Taniqua brought her daughter to the window for the first time to see the sun as it became visible over Toronto.

"Look at the sun", she said to her daughter with tenderness in her voice.

"The sun is coming up mommy", Tanisha said from her observation.

"The sun is not coming up babe; the earth is moving. The sun does not move", Taniqua said to correct her daughter's interpretation of sunrise. "They say sunrise but the sun stays in one place all the time".

"It is orange and red and yellow. I like green better. Green is my favorite color. What is your favorite color mommy?

"Blue"

"But blue is for boys"

"You can love any color you want". She took a deep breath and soaked up the scenery one more time before going back to the table to finish eating breakfast. "Come on; let's eat, we have a long day ahead of us. Happy birthday", she told her daughter again with a safe tight hug.

"Congratulation to you mama, I love".

"Are you always going to call me Mama?

"No MOM!

As they were cleaning up the apartment Tanisha asked,

"Mom, why did the sun come up at our window this morning? It was never there before"

"Because it is your birthday and God wants to say good morning and that He remembers your birthday. He is saying happy birthday".

"Thank God", she said with gratitude, looking through the window. What about last time; why did He not say happy birthday then?

"It was cloudy. The clouds were in His eyes"

"Do you know that it is Jesus?

"What?

"The sun"

"Jesus is stronger that the sun. He is not in the sun. He is where no one can see Him. Oh! I understand what you're trying to say. Jesus is God's son but not the sun that we can see"

"Is he playing Marco Polo with the angels? She asked without caring about her mother's attempt to explain her question.

"I think He is playing Esau, Esau, yes Jacob. I guess He could be playing any of the two"

Tanisha looked a bit perplexed, Is He playing with His father or the angels?

"They are all playing together. They do everything together"

"They are not like daddy; he does not do much with us anymore"

"I'm sorry babe. Do you know who is coming to your party and I do not mean your friends?

"Tommy?

"No"

"Who?

"Jesus and all the angels will be there. They like to have fun at parties"

"I'm not a baby, mama. I am six years old. God do not go to birthday parties. You're just being silly"

"Why not?

"If they are at my party; who will take care of the sun and the moon and the animals and the traffic so that daddy can come to my party", Tanisha clarifies her statements.

There was a knock on the door. "Oh Lord, please let it not be Tommy", Taniqua wished with dread.

"Why mama? Don't you like him?

The loud thump broke their conversation. "Shhh! He will go away"

The thump was heavier on the door then the knob turned. Taniqua was getting a bit scared as it appeared that the person on the other side of the door was trying to unlock the door. She had changed the lock on the door, so it could not be Duquan. Both stood in silence with suspense when the door cracked opened. The chain was on the door to hinder the person from coming in. There was a long pause at both ends then a loud call followed by three rapid bangs on the door.

"Taniqua! Taniqua!

"DADDY! You are here on my birthday", Tanisha exclaimed as she ran to open the door for her father without getting her mother's permission. He picked her up in his arms. "You remembered my birthday"

"You are my girl; I will always remember your birthday"

"You're early for the party"

He put her down and showed her a plastic bag, "I brought you breakfast from Mickie D"

"What's that?

"McDonald! You're a silly goose"

Taniqua spoke up so that he would acknowledge her presence. "Now I see where she gets that silly goose from. We just had breakfast together".

"Morning"

"Yeah"

"Do you want some?

"I am full. How did you get a key for the door?

"From the office. I told them I lost my copy and they gave me a copy"

"I gave them specific instructions not to give anyone a copy. Not even the likes of you".

He interrupted her, "Sorry. Is it ok to have breakfast with my girls?

"What about your sons who are almost awake?"

"Today is for both of you and I want to be a part of that"

Tanisha was already at the table helping herself. "Save some for daddy and mommy", Duquan told her.

"I cannot eat it all silly!

"Save some for your brothers and sister too", Taniqua added.

"I will. I like McDonald Hash Browns daddy"

"Daddy knows child"

"Daddy knows child; are you smoking something? Don't answer that. Whatever you're up to, don't".

This is Awkward.

Flower Among Ash

Duquan took the children by their grandmother's house where the celebration will be held later. Taniqua had time to do some laundry and catch up with her housework. It is not that she wanted to do all that dusting and cleaning but she was keeping herself busy because of anxiety. She tried hard to calm her nerves but nothing she did help. She had not heard from Ingrid or Ketrel and had called it a lost for her best friends. She pondered and wondered and paced the room until she had nothing else left to do.

"They probably will show up at the graduation to surprise me", she thought to herself. "Or maybe they forget or maybe they will be at the party", she got carried away in her thoughts. "Maybe Duquan took the kids and they are not by my moms and later I have to celebrate alone. I have to call mama". She called her mother. "Mama, are the children there? Just checking! I am fine. I am going to get dress now. I won't be late mama, the TTC will do. I have a token. I was hoping that Ketrel would take me but he has not call me in days, don't worry; I'll find my way. Yes! Yes, mama, I should go now. Remember I am taking the subway. Ok. See you later then! Bye", she sighs with relief knowing her children will be there later to celebrate. "It will be fun. Fun, fun, fun! she assured herself.

She was leaving the apartment when she saw Tommy coming off the elevator. She could not re-enter the apartment because the door was already closed. He looked into her direction.

"WOW! You look foxy mama", he complimented her.

"No one uses the word *foxy* anymore"

"Well, babe, you are bringing it back baby! he said trying to flatter her.

"You are trying too hard Tommy", she told him as she made her way past him.

"Don't you want your man to try hard to keep you?

"Whatever"

"Should I bring something to the party? Speaking with a fake British accent.

"Please stop", she said trying to keep back her smile.

"C'mon! Show me them pearls."

The elevator door was about to close when he said the words she wanted to hear. "I can give you a lift to the graduation. It will take me one minute to change. It is raining cats and dogs outside and I do not want my sweets, my chocolate dumpling to melt"

She came out of the elevator and followed behind him. "I would like to know who you are hanging out with to misinform you about black people slang and culture. I hope you do not act this way in public"

After opening the door, he responded to her., "Why not?

"It is embarrassing"

"Some people think it is amusing"

"They are lying to you; trust me"

He invited her in the apartment. she hesitated. "I want you to trust me by coming inside and wait for me", he spoke like he was talking to a small child. "It will only take one minute and with all the robbery going on, I do not want to keep my door open. I am not ghettoized fully yet to defend myself"

She stepped inside, "You are so misinformed about people living here. Anyways, make it quick!

They were leaving Tommy's apartment when they saw Duquan about to enter Taniqua's apartment. He saw them and stood there in astonishment. "What is this? What is going on?

"What does it seams like? I am going to my graduation", Taniqua replied in haste and headed for the elevator.

Tommy walked after her quickly and silently. Duquan caught up with them as they waited for the elevator.

"Was that the afternoon's guilty pleasure that the milk dud gave you? He asked. No one responded. "Little Tommy, hear this, this is where you get off".

"Get off what? The elevator?

"This is my woman, so shake like a tree and leave"

"He is giving me a ride to graduation", Taniqua tried to explain

"Have you not had enough in his apartment?

Taniqua felt insulted. "You know what? I do not have to explain myself to you. This goes to show you how much you do not know me". The elevator came and they all went on. She held the door opened, "Please leave Duquan. It is raining and I am going with Tommy which is none of your business".

He did not respond to Taniqua but sternly looked at Tommy and spoke clearly to him to avoid misinterpretation. "There in no room for hitchhikers Tommy boy. She is my baby mama so you better get off or I will ......

"What are you going to do boy? I am not afraid of you", Tommy replied in a confrontational manner.

He was not about to back down and Taniqua did not want things to escalade. "Thanks Tommy for being a gentleman in offering me a ride but this is my day and I do not want to witness any crime".

"Are you sure?"

"Yes"

"Don't let me have to talk to you about this again, BOY!

Tommy walked out of the elevator with regret. "See you later"

"Later! NEVER", Duquan interjected.

Out-doing Each Other

Flower Among Ash

Duquan escorted Taniqua to her mom's home. When they got home, their families and guests were huddling and enthralled by what was going on. They did not notice them coming inside the house.

"Hey everybody! Time to start the party! I am here!" Taniqua announced her entrance. They did not budge. "Hello everyone, I am here", she persisted without and success. Their laughter drowned out her voice.

Ketrel was on the outskirt of the huddle. Duquan tap him on his shoulder.

"What's going on man?

"Hey buddy! I never knew that this guy was so funny", he answered.

Ketrel did not finish replying to Duquan's question when Tommy stood up in the center of the crowed and greeted him. "Hey pal! Your mother-in-law is such a nice person. What took you so long? By now Taniqua was standing there on pins and needles. The tension between the three was intense when Tommy broke the ice. "The cake is so good. This is the first time I'd ever eaten Jamaican black cake. Come and join the fun. The children are watching a movie in the bedroom. I got that Horton hears a Hooo-whoever". In disbelief Taniqua took the slice of cake Tommy handed her and joined in the fun half-heartedly. Ingrid had showed up but the relationship between the two was still estranged.

Taniqua went into the kitchen for the match to light the candles on Tanisha's cake when Duquan walked in behind her and demanded her to throw Tommy out. "How long are you going to let him stay here?

"Him? That does not say much", she replies knowing full well what he meant.

"I bet by now you smell like his armpit the way you've been rubbing up on him"

"I was being polite"

"Really?

"Your daughter invited him and my mom seems to be enjoying his company and so are the other guests"

"I want him gone"

"I am not going out there to spoil my daughter's party"

"This is not about Tanisha! It is about you smooching with pale face. What did happen in the apartment earlier?"

Taniqua walked away and left him standing there in the kitchen. He followed after her and as he was in earshot of everyone, he spoke distinctly, "Let me take this from you my sweets. Today is your day and our first child's day too. Have a seat and let me serve you both". He walked her over to the dining table and seated her with the mannerism of a gentleman. He then pulled out a chair next to her and indicated to Tanisha to sit on his lap. He continues to speak so that all in the room could hear him.

"This is just a taste of things to come babe, just you and me and our children. Tommy! Hey Tommy! Do me a favour and play with your new best friend. You are the only adult I know to take an invitation from a little girl to go to a party". He laughed hysterically and looked for confirmation from Taniqua. He tried to make out with her but she outwardly refused.

Tommy walked over to them and spoke to her in a persuasive tone, "Don't leave me hanging; unless you are saving the last dance for us'" he said without looking at Duquan.

Duquan got into his face but Ketrel intercepted him.

Flower Among Ash

They all tried to calm him down but he would not budge until Tanisha yelled, "DADDY!, you are spoiling my birthday party! STOP! Stop messing up my party".

Taniqua's mother asked Duquan to leave but he promised to be on his best behaviour. Tommy went in the kitchen and insisted to help Taniqua's mom clean up. The mood of the party died and Taniqua went into the spare bedroom to put her boys to sleep when Ketrel walked in. "Quite an interesting night? Is there something going on with you and Tommy?

"Do not start with me"

"Just asking. Duquan seemed to be guarding you all night like a vulture over dead meat"

"At his convenience all the time. I will not live under his thumb. Is this the way he is going to behave should I want to move on with someone who truly cares for me?

"You meant Tommy?

"Is he the only man on earth that would show interest in me?

"He is the only one in this house who does; looking at you like some raw meat"

"At least he was looking"

"I do not think it is wise to encourage such a relationship because....

"I am through letting Duquan run my life. If you want your friend to stay out of prison, tell him to get off by back"

She was about to walk out when he held her on her wrist, "I admire what you have done with your life and all. I wish Ingrid were more like you. To be honest, I wish so many times we had a family and...

"Ketrel don't"

"I just want you to know that I am proud of you and the way you turned your life around. Thanks for the support. You are a classy babe and I know one day soon, you are going to leave all of us in the ghetto. I envy Duquan but I wanted you and him to work things out, for the children sake. I am sticking by Ingrid because of my children and I was hoping you two do the same"

"Do you love her?

"It is about my children"

"That is not enough for me"

"I know. That is why I love you"

"What?

"As a good person; love you like a friend. You have dreams like I did in school," he said trying to cover the slip of his lips.

"Put all that energy in keeping your friend from me because this time I will be the one sending him to prison".

Ingrid walked in, "Who is going to prison?

Taniqua gave her the dirty look and left the room. Thanks for coming", she said to her sarcastically as they passed by the doorway. They followed behind her just as Tommy had finished cleaning up in the kitchen. Taniqua's mother excused herself and went to bed. Taniqua put a CD in and asked Tommy to dance with her. She was pushing Duquan' button and he exploded. She threatened to call the police and with Ketrel's help, things were at a standstill until Taniqua's mom came out after Tanisha ran into the room whaling her head off. The party ended prematurely. Taniqua stayed overnight to prevent any further confrontations. It was the first-time Tanisha was not eager to say goodnight

Flower Among Ash

to her father. Although Duquan begged to see her before he left but she ignored him.

It was well passed midnight when her phone rang. "Hello. Sorry I cannot talk right now. You or anyone else. I do not want to start anything with you Ingrid! It is just as I said. Thanks for showing up! What else do you want me to say? Whatever. Goodnight. It meant just that! Thanks for showing up. Why am I being like this? Dah! Don't you have something better to do? We are not friends anymore so I am going to hang up now so…..if you do not know why I am acting this way according to you, then I cannot help. No, you are the one that broke our friendship? I am tired so good night. YES! That is how it is going to be! It was your decision. NO! You said I acted as if I was better. You are the one who had changed but you know what; you are jealous". She hanged up the phone. "Oh my gosh! Can this night get any worst?" The doorbell rang immediately. "I spoke too soon"

"Who is it?" her mother asked from her room.

She looked through the window next to the door, "It is Tommy! She told her mother. "What do you want?

"I forgot to give you the gift I bought you. You do not have to open the door fully"

She opened the door and took the gift. "Thanks".

"I hope you like it. I have the receipt; if you do not like it, I can return it"

"What is it?

"Open it! If you do not like it, I will get you another one in the morning?

She opened the little box and gasped. "WOW! I love

it." Her reflexive muscles threw her arms around him hugged him.

"De rien. You are welcome"

"I know what you meant; I too did some French in school"

"Goodnight then, Tommy".

"I am glad you like it. Just know you can count on me to be here for you whenever you want", Tommy said to her.

"I appreciate it but I'll be ok".

Here we are Again

Flower Among Ash

Taniqua came full circle to another sweltering summer in her dilapidated apartment. The paint was peeling as usual and the cupboards doors were falling off their hinges. In addition to the unhealthy apartment, the garbage cans three floors down, under her window made it unbearable to open her window, but what's new. Not that it would help. The heat outside was suffocating as the dry air in the apartment.

This time there were a lot of boxes and garbage bags piled up in the living room. She was packed and ready to move out of the apartment. She was moving close to her job in the Bathurst and Finch area. This was a big step up for her since she had graduated. Her life was beginning to move forward towards her goal to leave her bad experiences behind.

One thing had changed. Duquan was coming around more often and sleeping over to keep Tommy away from Taniqua. Their usual arguments penetrated the walls. At one point, the neighbor had to call the police. Today is emotional for her. The transition was not going to be easy.

She knew that Duquan would not have access to her new place. He pleaded with her and when that did not work, he argued. She was saying goodbye to old habits and picking up the pieces of her broken heart. She had waited for the man she loved so long to come around and return her love. Times she had wasted waiting for him to commit to her and his children was lost.

She was packed and ready to go. Duquan watched helplessly. She poured her heart out to him again but this time she had more control. In her weakness; she was strong. Her speech was coherent.

I've been here before.
Grappling at your feet,
Begging you to love me.
For you to care!
I have been here before
With you
Begging you to love and care for your children
I've been here before,
Last year,
You were on top
And I
Subjected myself to you.
I have been here where
You
Got tired of me and threw me out like a used paper towel
TODAY
Here I am telling you
That I will rise from the ash of your neglect
It over for us
it is the start of a brighter future
For me
And my kids
Here I am again
With you
Between these two same doorposts
Saying to you
I am through with your games.
This is only the beginning,
It is a guarantee,
I will not turn back
This is the end of our story Duquan.

He responded calmly, "You were always poetic in high school. You also did well in Drama. Taniqua. I admit, I was wrong. I took you for granted. I cannot believe you went back to school and worked part time and look at you now. So, I was jealous and I still do not like the way you showed me up".

She interrupted him, "How did I show you up?

"Let me finish. You had your say now it is my time. I listen to your poetic justice presentation so…

OK! I am listening!

"Anyways. I lost my thought, oh. As I was saying, you'd showed me up by going to school without asking me.

"Excuse me. Ask you"

"I said let me finish. You made me look bad before Ingrid saying I can't control my woman and how you were infiltrating your ideas on her. She was ticked off when Ketrel started going to school saying I should put a leash on you and things like that. I wear the pants in this family so I was not going to support that at all, you know what I'm saying.

Taniqua was livid. "You listened to her and break up our family. In the first place, you never wear the pants for this family. You seldom worked. Your children were hungry many times. Look at Tanisha who adores you. Since the party, it is like you do not exist to her. You let that woman tell you what to do and the woman that should matter most to you, you ignored. They could tell you what to do, which you did, while I was just asking you to be a father to your kids and show me some respect. I am not going to even get heated over what Ingrid told you because she has no future. She is satisfied with settling but I cannot. Not anymore. I need to change the people I hang out with. As they say, friends are like elevators, they can take you up or down and that is why I am counting you as a lost"

"I thought you and Ketrel were tight"

"We are but I will not hang out with him to get tangled with this mess again"

"You said that Tanisha is still upset at me since her birthday, how am I to make it up to her if I do not know where you live?

"Pick them up at my mom"

"I guess I deserve this. Will you be hooking up with pale face?

"That is none of your business, besides, I am not man crazy. I've matured. It took me a long time to get where I am now but the fact is I am here. I tell you, I went through hell with you, waiting for you. Boy! What was I thinking?

"Marry me then"

"Pardon"

"You heard me. Marry me. Let us get married"

"How romantic. I am getting ready to leave you permanently and you want me to marry you. Marry me then, he said", she repeated in disbelief.

"I want to marry you", he repeated. "For our children's sake", he added.

"No. You want to marry me now that someone else wants to be with me. You never knew that one day I would leave you. Well, that day is here"

"We have four children together"

"Now you can count"

He went down on one knee and asked, "Will you marry me, please? I have been a jerk but things will change. Look at you. You have change and so can I. Give me another chance, please. Don't let me beg"

"Why not?

"Will you say yes?

"I have been here before"

"I'd never asked you to marry me before"

"I know but I meant that we had come to a point when you decided to be serious about me and the kids then you renege your promise and it always happen when you think you are going to lose me. Since I am that important to you, why the run around?

"I mean it this time"

"I cannot deal with this roller coaster ride. I am only working fulltime until January then I will be going back to school to become a Dentist. My employer suggested that I have the natural gift for dentistry so I will be tied up with no time to spear for your mess".

"Don't you just graduate? You, a dentist? Not because you were lucky to graduate that does not mean that you can be a dentist. Not everybody can be a dentist"

"That is showing me you have not changed. You will never support me and my goal. You think very little of me. Why not me? Why can I not be a dentist?

"You are suddenly bold. Before school, you were submissive to me"

"I was a fool then"

"Who is going to help you with all the moving"

"I did not fall from the sky; I have family. I have weaned you. You were about to close the casket on me eh! Thought I was washed up and would never be somebody. You thought I was going to be your yoyo all the days of my life, waiting around for you when it was convenient for you. You even thought I was going to drop out of school when you chose not to support my decision in going back to school. I did it without your help. Now I am moving on. Get with it".

"I want to get with you"

"I can do better"

"Really?

"Much better than you. The moving truck and the guys are downstairs. Please excuse me".

"Let me help".

"If you do, I will personally call the police. Bye Duquan".

Back Pew Ministry, "Pastors are sinners too"

Taniqua had a lot on her mind. Her life had changed. She had found success in her education and wanted to continue learning. Her eyes have been opened to many possibilities. Education was the only thing she was good at, where she had control and feels good about being somebody. With the usual distractions with her and Ingrid, her mind wonders what to do about Duquan. She searched for answers through prayer and ask God for directions. She wanted to do right by her children but the thought of letting go of her friends and Duquan was heart wrenching.

She had tolerated him far too long. She had become the person she could not recognize. Even now, she is still astounded by the fact that she got a certificate, which opened the doors to better living. Unlike Ketrel, her companions were settling for mediocre living while she wrestles with discontentment. It was as if the universe was speaking to her, causing her to feel uncomfortable in her situation. Now she battles with the decision, should she drop her friends of many years permanently or drag them along?

Education had changed her. Her income was because of answered prayers. She sat by herself on the balcony where the young people sat during church service with just a few elderly members supervising.

Two women who are trying to find their age came to sit in front of her. Then another came and joins them. "Sister Inez, come and sit with us because things are not right in this church", Louise beckoned to her.

"You here what happened to pastor and his wife? Rumour has it..." Mary announced with excitement.

"Let me sit first". She made herself comfortable. "So

the church is going to the dogs now? We should have an emergency board meeting to read him out of the church"

"Out of the conference", Mary added.

"Do not keep me in the dark", Inez interjected. "Update me. The last thing I heard was that the associate pastor was going to leave the church to go to America and leave his wife"

"He is using it as an excuse. He is not going there for ministries. Immigration turned them down and he wants to go to America to find another woman to get his green card. That is the entire story and I heard it form good source. Pastor wife's cousin told me to pray for the pastor and his wife because immigration did not approve their application".

"I know you got the 411 sister Inez. I think these foreign pastor use ministries to get a visa. It is not about God. Now the poor woman must go back to Guyana all by herself while he goes off to America to preach the good news. Long distance relationship will destroy their marriage. He is a man like anybody else and prone to sin".

"You said it sister Mary", Louise agreed. "Who knows, he might already have his eyes on somebody over there. And you know these young people", Mimicking a childish talk, "Happy Sabbath pastor, hi pastor, how are you pastor and touching him here and there. These young pastors need more discipline. They are too close to these young girls, acting friendly and all".

"I was shocked when he made the announcement last week that he was leaving and his wife was going home to Guyana. I was sorry for the poor soul. The tears she shed were not because she was going home but that he was

Flower Among Ash

leaving her for America. He forgot what revelation says about America?

"Sister Louise, it is all about getting the green card".

"But Inez, he is the pastor. That is not true?

"Maybe he is modern day Jonah".

"Sister Mary, don't be naive".

"Tell me the truth behind the senior pastor and his daughter? Sister Mary asked with naivety.

The two-women jaw dropped opened and their eyes bulged out of their heads.

"You did not hear?

"No! The two reply in unison

"Apparently, she got pregnant at the church school college in America and when she came back home he kicked her out of the house. Some said he kicked her out when he found out she was active sexually but others said that it is because the beans got spilled why he did it as to show he does not condone her action".

"It is like taking action after the horse got through the gate"

"You are right sister Inez. But looking at it, I am glad that she didn't abort it to cover her sins knowing that her father is a minister".

"Lord have mercy! What are you telling us? Inez asked with intense curiosity.

"Or disguise it as miscarriage. She is not the first or the last to go away to school and end up in situations like this".

"No matter what, sin is sin. She fornicated and it caught up with her. I wonder if the pastor is covering up his daughter's sin. How much he knows and what? I will not tolerate this in my church." Inez spoke with authority.

"What is happening to the church? Being the devil's advocate; he has a lot on his plate. The young people in this church need the blood of Jesus to literally cleanse them. What has this world come to. The temptation is worst than when we were growing up".

"It is the shaken. God is cleansing his church sister Louise".

"It has been four months and she is not showing so I guess she had an abortion".

"How could you say that Mary? You know that he talked Dinah from having an abortion even though she is in her thirties. Give him what is due; he is not like that. The world is going on a faster pace and temptation is more intoxicating than ever".

"Have you heard the saying? Have many friends and treat them well but never to them your secret tells, for when your friends become your foe, out in the world your secret goes. His secret is all over the church".

"Exposed", they agreed.

"Well that is what happened. The person that took her to the doctor exposed her. I heard that she was trying to take back her words. The two had a brief fall out and that is why everybody knows. It is too late now; their relationship has been severed. I hear pastor was upset because that same girl eats and sleeps at their home and he feels she is the one that encourage his daughter into premarital sex".

"The person who accompanied her to the doctor; how did they know about this doctor of ill repute? Unless that person had an abortion too. Think about it. I am glad that she didn't go through with it. She is going to need Jesus to get through this. I remember when I was expecting my son.

Being an unwed parent felt like I was branded or scar with the label trash on my forehead. Putting all this rumor aside, the pastor did make my life easier. He helped and always made sure that I had food. It shows that bad things happen to good people and children do not always follow in the footsteps of their parents"

"Sister Inez, I never thought of it that way. You are unto something. I think he is blaming her. Probably he knew that she wanted to do it. He must be infuriated"

"Maybe they should give these girls that go away to college birth control pills and the boys' condoms", Taniqua said rudely interrupting the women. "Primitive Christians like you refrain from talking about birth control to young people but it is not hard to talk about abortion and murder base on weak assumptions. That's what you are implying. Which is better? The death of an unborn child or preventative method? And what about those who carry their children to full term? And another thing, who died and make you judge and jury over us. People are flesh and the flesh will sin. And by the way, you three are sinners too. Beware of your uncontrollable tongue on the Lord's house; it might condemn you. It is people like who are stumbling block to sincere people from coming to God. And by the way, the pastor has no control over his daughter's decision. He is expecting her to live per the principles he taught her. Nonetheless, Christ never condemn or judge us, He restore us to Himself. Open the Bible every now and then, you all might be converted".

The women got up and walked away before she could finish.

Taniqua sighed, "We are a mess God, please fix us"

Goodbye Mr. Sandbox; One Last Dig

Flower Among Ash

Taniqua went back to the apartment to collect the rest of her belongings and to clean up the apartment for the next tenant. It was if Duquan was watching the apartment for her to return to get the rest of her things. He gladly helped her cousins with the heavy lifting but was very disappointed when he was told that they no longer required his help.

She felt relieved and stopped by the sandbox to play with her children. It was the first time in a long time she was submerged in what her children were doing while enjoying their company. Her laughter came from a re-ignited soul.

She was not keeping track of the time because she was saying farewell to her past. Joyous tears streaked down her face as she realised her dreams to leave this part of town had come to fruition. Something she thought would never happened to her. She went across to the convenient store to get some snacks then returned to the sandbox to eat with her children.

She saw Tommy out of the corner of her eye and tried not to look into his direction. He walked over and sat down into the sandbox next to her. "Is this your final day?

"Yep!

"You will be missed"

"I am not going to miss this place"

"What about me?

"Why should I miss you?

"Wow. I never expected that"

"Well, that is life. It is unpredictable"

"Keep in touch"

"If I have the time. My mom lives far and Ingrid and I are not close as we were before, so, I am doing this all by myself. I have an uncle that lived near by but he is of very little help. His wife says she will help with the kids when she can and my mom, you know her. She is finally proud of me. As you see I will be very busy working and all"

"You do not have to give me a sermon to give me the brush off"

"If that is what you call it"

"It is a nice area"

"Yeah, it is. The apartment is expensive but it is the cost of living in that part of the city"

"Be careful you do not end up here again"

"Why would you say that?

"I am not wishing you bad and all but if you are going to do this on your own, the rent will be a challenge for you"

"Do not concern yourself. I have my Jesus"

"So you did not have Him before?"

"Probably not"

"I wish you well"

"I am working. It pays well"

"I guess with your income and the child support you will be getting from Duquan, that will do the trick".

"You are trying to know my business! I am fine. I will be Ok. I am doing right by myself and my children this time"

"Is it over with you and Duquan?

"That is personal"

"You are a bit tight lip today"

"Because you are inquiring of my past which I am not willing to discuss with you or anyone else. Tommy, look at me, I am happy. I have a sense of contentment and accomplishment. I want to keep this aura around me now and always"

"Can I come and visit?

Flower Among Ash

"No"

"Why not?

"I will not jump from relationship to another in such a short time. I need time for my children and myself. I am re-establishing myself".

"You are going to drop me like a hot potato"

"I never had you"

"We could have something going. You know how I feel about you"

"Thanks"

"Thanks! Thanks, and that's it?

"There is nothing more I can say. It may sound cold but if you know where I am coming from; you would understand"

"You're going to let one bad relationship turn you away from every guy?

"I am twenty-three. I have been with Duquan since I was sixteen. I am entitled to some man free moments without apologies. I know you mean well but now is not a good time for me"

"This is where you say it is not you, it is me"

"I don't have to. I must go now. You take care of yourself".

"You know my address. Come by when you have time".

"Bye Tommy".

"You make it sound like forever"

"I can tell you this; I will try my best not to come back here. Why don't you go back to Rosedale? You should understand why people move on to find themselves or to achieve what they want".

"Look me up. I am in the book".

The hugged and went their separate ways.

She Got What She Wanted

Flower Among Ash

Taniqua was busy setting up the room for the next patient when the next patient. She gathered all the tools the doctor will be using when the patient came in the room. Without looking at the person, she spoke. "Make yourself comfortable; the doctor will be with you in a minute. You will need this". She handed her the pair of glasses. She realized that the woman was pregnant. "How far along are you?

"Twenty-two weeks".

"Are you going to find out the sex of your baby? She asked trying to make small talk.

"I want to. I would be elated if it is a boy".

"I thought women prefer girls"

"My boyfriend has two girls so I would like to give him the child that will carry his name"

"Sounds like a fairy tale to me", she replied.

"Your voice sounds familiar to me. Where do you live?

"Just up the road"

"I am trying to figure out where we might have met"

"I might look like someone you have met. These days I am so busy with the children and work. I am trying to work as much overtime as possible. I thought after I'd moved form Parkdale….

She jumped up with excitement, "I lived in Parkdale once and I gave my furniture to….

"Robin! Wow!

"It is you!

Are you carrying the baby of that guy?

"YES! I got my man, partially. I got a condo in the Yonge and Finch area and that is why I want a boy to do the final trick. He wants a son so badly"

"Did you drug him?

"I charmed him with my thick lips and wide hips"

"You are full of yourself"

"No, I love myself. You moved to this neighbourhood. The last time I saw you, you were pining after that guy"

"Well, I went back to school. And here I am with a skill and living it up here, scrambling to make things work but I'm not complaining"

"Where is the man?

"Where I left him"

"We have one thing in common"

"What is that?

"We want better".

"I am doing it the harder and the right way. I cannot believe you went through with your plan. I was so out of it that day when you gave me your furniture. My head is still spinning from your generosity. But to break up a family. I felt bad for taking your furniture after knowing what you were about to do"

"The wife is one of those women who sleeps in a different room from her husband. She does her thing and he does his. He had needs and I was there for him. The condo was to keep the wife in the dark and to give us more private time together. He was so deprived but not anymore. I might have twins. Wouldn't it be great to have twin boys?

"What if he does not marry you?"

"Then I will keep on trying or go to plan B"

"And what is plan B?

"To tell his wife and her mother. I have their phone numbers. I know where the mother lives. I think if I get to the mother-in-law, she would push for her daughter to get a divorce. If that does not work; I will not allow him to see his children".

"Come on! Not the children".

"I am praying for boys. He has been with me for every doctor's visits. He is paying for my visit here. Things are ruling in my favour. Look at you. You made it. Good for you! I am proud of you".

"Thanks".

"You are just like me. You know what you want and goes after it".

"I guess we will be running into each other in the future. Please take care of yourself and try not to end up in Parkdale again".

"I won't".

The doctor walked in and interrupted the two, "It everything ready?

"Ready and waiting".

Kiss and Ride

"Why are you loitering outside my mom's house? You are supposed to drop the children off and go your ways. What are you waiting for? It has been nearly three months since I left Parkdale and all the rodents that comes with living there. Don't you get the message by now, I am avoiding you! I have no time for this game you want to play. I have moved on. There is no place in my life for you Duquan. You and your friends claim I am a hypocrite and acting holier than thou so please leave me alone so you guys will not have to feel inferior. I have put away childish thing and living the way that pleases God and me. Please, when you drop the children off, leave, capeesh"

"I wanted to see you. You look different in your uniform. Who is the guy that dropped you off?

"Go chase your tail Duquan"

"You are really not going to take me to court for child support?

"Where were the law when we were making those children? If you cannot love and support your children freely; so be it"

"I know women do not make a lot of dough, you must need some help"

"You have trouble with foot-mouth-disease. Help from you leads to confusion and ungodly living. Get it through your thick skull, I have had enough. My mom told me you just sit around here in the streets with the children. You are supposed to pick them up and take them at your place or wherever, then bring them back here. This is the drop off and pick up point. Why am I doing this?

"Can we go somewhere and talk?

"Talk about what? I gave you my innocence, my

childhood and my dignity. I became the person I hated so much. I will never let you drag me there again"

"Ketrel was asking about you. Ingrid is alone. She misses the company"

"You are their spoke person now?

"I came by the church and you were not there. I have been there almost every week. The pastor preaching was alright".

"I have been visiting other churches with likeminded people. Apparently, I have been going to the extreme to break away from the pack. It has been working and will remain that way"

"What if we got married?

"You are a lost cause. Marrying you is going back to the past. I am moving forward"

"What if I got baptize?

"Do not get baptize for me. Do it for yourself"

"I need you in my life. I will do anything for you"

"Need. You need me in your life. Really! You know, getting baptize won't help when you are not clearly converted"

"How do I get converted?

"The fact that you're asking me that means you are not. Get some Bible lessons until the Spirit of God speaks to you. You are so far from God right now. You cannot go to church for the soul purpose to be with me. The church is not a dating, match making service, it is the place you go to when you are sick and tired of your sinful life and to get relief and hope to be with Christ when He returns. I am not a Bible worker. I cannot help you. Only God can"

"Study the Bible with me"

Flower Among Ash

"When you go back to the church looking for me, tell the pastor that you are interested in Bible lessons and he will take it from there"

"Why can't we study together?

"You have the wrong agenda"

"How do you know that? I am sincere"

"Good for you"

"You are judging me. Only God can read what is in my heart"

"Also action speaks louder than words. Whatever spirit rules your life can be seen by your actions. You need some alone time with God, not me. Goodnight".

"Help me find my way then"

"There will be too many conflicts. My ride is here. I must go. If you are truly looking for God, you will find him. Goodnight"

"Who is the dude picking you up? Is that your new man now? I see why you do not want to help me".

"Get help somewhere else; I cannot help you"

"Is that the reason why you have not been to church lately?

"What did I say to you earlier? This is what I am trying to avoid"

"Let me take you home"

"So you can know where I live"

"Is that so bad? He knows where you live. I bet he is rolling in the sack with you while you're acting like you're serving God"

"I hope you look real hard for God because you would have to, to find Him and for God to penetrate that thick skull of yours. This is all about being jealous"

"God is jealous, isn't He?

"Goodnight".

"Seen Tommy lately? I bet you are keeping in touch with him.

Tis the Season to be Jolly

Flower Among Ash

It has been a while since Taniqua had been to her home church. She decided to visit because it was a high day at church. It was Christmas. She was greeted by her old classmate from high school who have gone on the church university in the States and graduated with honors. Taniqua was not ashamed to greet her at the entrance.

She spoke with confidence, "Hi! How are you? It has been a while since I've seen you"

"Hi to you too! Where have you been?

"Here and there"

"Are you expecting again?

"No"

"It's that we have not seen you for a long time and we thought you were; you know what I mean".

"As you see, I am not", Taniqua replied feeling embarrassed.

"Glad that things are working out for you"

"I am the flower among the ash. People would give up on me, but here I am, flourishing"

"And to imagine we were in the same grades at high school and all, Wow!

"Well, I am a dental assistant now and I will be studying to become a dentist in the future starting next month. It's never too late".

"Being an Educator is was all I wanted to become. It's a coveted career"

"Educators do need to see the dentist, even the dental assistance"

"My family dentist is in Mississauga"

"Who knows, one day I will be the one handling your files"

"I guess someone has to do the filing"

"I am going inside now. Nice talking to you", Taniqua said and excused herself. "When are people going to stop dumping on me", she whispered to herself. As she entered the sanctuary, she bumped into Ingrid on her way to the washroom. They shared a quick hello. She went and sat with her family during Bible class. She tried not to get up but she had no choice but to go out and changed DJ's diaper. Duquan saw her and followed her into the mother's room.

"I saw the senior pastor just a minute ago going into his office. It is the opposite way", she told him.

"I do not need to see the pastor", he replied.

"I guessed you've not started Bible study", she asked.

"No"

"Why the change of heart? I was expecting you to be baptize by now"

"You are looking so hot"

"Thanks"

"Miss me?

"Not really"

"I cannot join the church unless I am certain you are coming back to me. I am the only one that can make your life better. It is time you stop fooling yourself and come back to me."

"I have already been dumped on; I am here in my son's poop, so please let me enjoy the day in peace. No more drama"

"I do not want any drama either. I just want a piece of my baby mama", he replied and slapped her on her bottom.

She picked up her half-dressed son and went inside. He followed her with a drunken grin on his face and squeezed himself into a space next to her in the pew. He sat beside her and burdened her shoulder with his heavy arm. She sat there through the entire service feeling embarrassed with the wordless public statement Duquan was making. To make matter worst, in the middle of the alter call, he kissed her ruggedly on her lips with a loud smack that echoed in the sanctuary. Wiping off her mouth only encouraged him to do it again. The pastor's eyes were fixed on them. This would be a good time for the earth to open and swallow her. She was not lucky enough. Everything else was a blur. She could only hear the thumping of her heart beating, as if it wanted to run away. She sat there until everyone trickled out of the sanctuary. Her mother took the children and went outside. He nibbled on her ears and that was when she snapped and slapped him in the face. She had never done that before and was shocked by what she had done. She had not seen that Ingrid and Ketrel were close by, but they were not close enough to prevent his reaction.

Before her next breath, he was on top of her hitting her and yelling, "Who is your man? Stop making a fool of me! No woman makes me look like an idiot! You hear me!

Ketrel and two deacons got him away from her. She lay on her back on the pew not wanting to see the crowd that reentered to sanctuary to see the blow by blow events. Ingrid sat down beside her to comfort her.

"I am so sorry"

"You brought him here. Are you happy now?

"I do not agree with what he has done"

"It does not matter. Now I know I have made the right choice"

"I know I have been a jerk but you cannot put this one on me"

"Is that your way of apologizing?

"For what? You left the group when you got your hot shot job"

"You were right Ingrid; I have changed"

Ketrel joined them, "Sorry T, if I'd know he was going to do that I would have given you the heads up"

She sat up, "But you didn't. Now, don't you understand why I had to drop your company. I am not like you guys. I was miserable and all you did, Ingrid, was to criticize me and you Ketrel have never stood up for me. All you were interested in was to save face for your dog. If he does not look bad about his woman leaving him. Did you ever care about me when you tried so desperately to keep us together? I do not think so. It was all about Duquan"

"Ketrel come on, you should have let Duquan….

"Do what? Smash my face in. You do not have to be jealous of me"

"K, let's get up on out of here before I do something I will regret", Ingrid said trying to pull Ketrel from the situation.

"You want to take a shot at me too? I will turn the other cheek to make it easy for you"

Ingrid was fuming at the mouth, "Through thick and thin I stood by your side babysitting"

"And since I went back to school?

"I am the person that help you get where you are right now?

"Thank you", Taniqua replied calmly. "Ketrel, how is school?

"Good".

"I wish you all the best. Have you noticed any recent changes lately in your relationship?

"Nothing more than the usual", he replied with naivety. "I have to make more time for her and school took up a lot of my time....

"And you should cut back", she said cutting him off. "I came by your place to keep in touch with you and both time you were not there. Are you quitting because your family gets in the way?

"You know I am not like Duquan. My family comes first at all times"

"Noble isn't Ingrid? If you do not want to improve yourself, do not keep the people you claim you love back but then again, did you tell me that you love Ketrel before you lived together or is it the other way around?

"Taniqua, I know it is obvious that it is over with you and Duquan but do not mess with my relationship. Misery loves company but here is where I draw the line".

"I won't, it is already a mess. I did nothing wrong. Going back to school and giving myself to God is what makes me happy. This is what helped me to choose my friends wisely. You are stuck in the past, past failures. If I have breath, I want better and that is living for Christ and your life style does not make room for me"

"Miss high and mighty. Don't forget where you are coming from"

"Goodbye Ketrel. Follow your heart. It is the only way to true happiness".

"I did not quit. I was on a leave of absence"

"Shut up Ketrel and stop sucking up to her, I am your

woman. If you ever think you are going to do like her and leave me, you're making a big mistake"

He watched Taniqua walked away, "That is one classy babe. I want to be like her", he whispered. "I have to go back to the program".

"What are you babbling to yourself?!, she yelled at him.

He looked at her with intensity, "I got stuck with the wrong woman", he told himself and walked away.

We wished Upon a Star

"How is she doing mam?

"She is lying down in her room. I don't think she is up for company. She is still distraught from what happened at church earlier. All I could do was to take the children to shield them from the madness"

"I won't stay long"

"Are you alone?

"Yes mam"

"Do me one favor"

"What is that?

"Don't drag my daughter in that mess again. Already she is second guessing pushing ahead with her studies and to become a dentist. She claimed it is too expensive but I know she is regressing into doubting herself. That man you called a friend took my little girl from me. She is trying to do right and I am putting down my foot".

"I am not here to hurt her or to ask her to mend fences, I just want to see how she is doing", Ketrel replied.

"Ok, but do not let me have to kick you out of my home or call the police"

"I am not a threat mam".

"Her room in on the right".

"I know, thanks".

He lay on the bed next to her without saying a word. They stared and the ceiling in silence. As they breathe alternately, he spoke. "How did you do it? The man is supposing to be the head but no matter how hard I try; I know how you feel now. I am starting to feel out of place with Ingrid and Duquan. I feel like I do not fit in. I want something better. She is not doing it for me anymore. She kept on complaining I am not going to clubs with her anymore; all the drinking and smoking pot. I don't know. All my life I thought I was ok doing odd jobs here and there; working for cash so welfare would not find out. You knew I dropped out of the program, didn't you? But I can still learn a lot more at the dealership. Thanks to you I am certified for drive clean and I am learning other tricks of the trade too. I am still climbing the ladder but differently. Ingrid started acting up as soon as I enrolled in the in the first class. I went home with good news and she just dragged me back to reality. A sad one. I tried but she made all the excuse to go out when I have classes or should study. My hat's off to you; you did it. I wish I had the courage like you. I just do not want to lose my children".

"More like a nervous breakdown", she finally spoke. "It was confusing trying to understand why I was growing apart from my friends that I have loved all my life. I was starting to believe I was becoming a snob. I did not know who I was becoming but I was sure that I was not in my niche and it felt horrible. I struggled with letting Duquan go; not only because I love him but I know I would have to break all ties with you and Ingrid; she made it easier. Since I started working as a dental assistant, my life has changed and it is not because of my salary. I went to my employer's home in Oakville twice. Once for his daughter's birthday and then his wife's. It is a huge mansion with indoor pool. I felt like a princess and it was not my house. My children are having a ball. We went to CNE, Marine Land, Canada's Wonderland, and Black Creek. To top it off; our staff dinner was at this fancy hotel downtown. His is deliberate in trying to opens my eyes to Toronto's culture and boy! My eyes are opened. I believe I have seen all the plays, ate at the best restaurants that I must dress up just to walk through the door. All this would have been going on around me, passing me by if I had not gone back to school. I truly understand when they say a new world open to you when you have some sort of skill or education. The strange thing is I feel like I belong; like the puzzle piece that was missing. I feel Disneyfied! If there is such a word. It is a dream and I am living it. I missed out on a lot".

"Dreams do come true".

"I think for people like us; we have to make our dream come true".

"You remember that part in the Lion King when the pig and that thing were looking up at the stars? I am looking at them now. I am looking for my wishing star. Back in Jamaica, whenever you seen a shooting star; you would make a wish"

"What was your wish?

"To come to Canada to my dad"

"You got your wish".

"Until the evil step-mother turned things around. She threw me out on the streets for no good reason and filled my father with lies. My family is always falling apart. My biological family and now my friends"

"Sorry"

Pointing to the ceiling, "Look at that one. It is the biggest"

"I do not, what are you looking at?

"Use your imagination", he insisted.

"I was beginning to think you have lost it". She closed her eyes, "I see it. Wow"

"I could lie here with you all day and look at the stars. Make a wish"

"I did. Did you?

"Yes. I cannot remember feeling at peace like I am now". He looks at her and saw that her eyes were closed. "Are you sleeping?

"No. Just star gazing"

"Try seeing them with your eyes open"

"She looked at him strangely, "I have never seen this side of you before".

"Go ahead! Look"

She stared at the ceiling until she announced with excitement," I see them! My heart is pounding"

"Isn't that a sight for sore eyes?

"Can I make another wish?

"I have made three wishes. The same one three times".

They gazed at the stars until their heavy eyelids silence their lips and they fell asleep. They slept together on the same bed and wished upon the same stars, the same wishes. When they got up, they both understood each other better and the path before them became clearer.

Yield Not to Temptation

Flower Among Ash

"Come in. How are you doing?

"So so"

"It is my day off; please excuse the mess that I am in"

"I have seen you in worst"

"Do you want something to drink? I have no alcohol. I have some carrot juice but it is made from boil carrot and beets"

"The place looks good and you look good as usual, even when you are a mess. Now that I can speak freely of how I feel about you; there are so many complications. Some days I do not know if I am coming or going. I have been thinking about the situation and cannot come up with a fair logical answer. It is as if I was destined to live miserably with Ingrid. What kind of a life is that for our children?

"You want the juice. I have not gone grocery shopping yet…there is not much I can offer you ".

"Thank you"

"Life is complicated. I have Hancock on DVD; you want to watch it?

"I guess"

"I bought a DVD! I am slow with technology but eventually I will catch up".

"You think Ingrid would ever cheat on me?

"I don't think so. She has her ways but, Nah!

"I guess that went through the window"

"What?

"I wanted an excuse for us to have one roll in the sack"

"It has been a very long time since I have been intimate with anyone but our friendship means too much to me to do such a thing. I know Ingrid and I are not on good terms at this moment but I could not do that to her".

"Why can't we try it one time? I am aching for you Taniqua. I am so thirsty to kiss your lips. I have been lusting after you for so long and now you and my dog is not kicking it, we cannot be together. It is very difficult for me to accept the fact we were never destined to be together"

"Here, have some juice. I could hear it in your voice on the phone but I ask you to come over because I either want to be with you or just want to be with somebody, anybody"

"You never had a thing for me?

"No"

"Why?

"I never saw you that way".

"Did you want to be with me in particular?

"You heard me. I wanted to be with someone"

"What about now?

"I am burning"

"Are we going to do it?

"Hmmmm?

"Are we going to do it? Ketrel repeated.

"I am going out of my mind right now"

"I have the cure"

"Please"

"Don't knock it until you try it'" he answered and they both laughed.

"I guess when they say the love of Christ constraints us is true because I still have those strong feelings but I am not able to act on them"

"Is it ok if I make the first move?

"I guess not"

"Yes or No? are you in any sort of contact with Duquan?

"He is the father of my children"

Flower Among Ash

"You guys getting back together?

"Not likely"

"He told me he wants to make it up with you but…

"He had many chances, besides he had me twisting like a pretzel for him. He was everything to me but now he means nothing to me"

"So we can?

"We have an history and besides I would not be able to look Ingrid in her face when I see her at church. Another thing, why is Ingrid so into going to church now when I had to drag her kicking and screaming to go with me?

"I will be going or else"

"Sometimes I wonder what you'd be like in bed"

"You have been thinking about me in that way! Taniqua said with astonishment.

"I know it is low but I have been having forbidden intimacy from my early teens now I am delirious because my situation forced me live without it and I can tell you; I have been lusting"

"We will let it die here, besides you will be getting it tonight"

"Everybody will be doing it except you, I can fix that"

"I know. And I would be a home wrecker. It is best if you go home now. This is not right. You would end up losing respect for me. I would have no respect for myself if we did anything stupid like that"

"Goodnight Taniqua", he said sadly.

"Goodnight Ketrel. We will forever remain good friends. See you later or maybe, never".

"Whatever you choose. Bye then".

Walking in Integrity

Flower Among Ash

Taniqua was entering the washroom to change DJ diaper after children's church when she ran into Ingrid. She greeted her mechanically.

"Hi Taniqua. Good to see you again".

"Yeah"

"DJ! You have grown", she said and leaned over to kiss DJ. "You must be walking and talking and doing all the little boys stuff" she said in a playful child's voice.

Taniqua continued to prepare the change table to change DJ's diaper. "How you've been?

"I see all the college thing paid off"

"Please don't go there".

"I hear you are back in school again"

"My boss said I should and he is paying fifty percent of the cost so I grab the opportunity and ran with it; and you?

"I am a stay home mom; you know that. I am not cut out for all that book stuff"

"Whatever you say"

"Ketrel told me that he was by your place last night"

Taniqua was now in the first stage of the Alarm Reaction. Unfortunately, her son was half naked which inhibited her from fleeing the scene. "He came by and we hang out for a bit" she hesitated trying to figure out what went down between them.

"You were always close and he respects you and all…I guess…I miss the old times"

Taniqua let out a sigh of relief, "He passes by every so often. We just kick it"

"Is there room for one more? She asked sheepishly.

In a shock state, Taniqua said to her' "I must say I missed you and the children"

"They missed their aunt and most of all, I miss you. So"
"I would hug you but I am elbow deep in poop"
"I am going inside. I'll save you a seat like old times?
"Sure, why not"

"The only thing I am requesting from you is that should we have a difference of opinion; we will not break our friendship. I love you and I miss you", she told Taniqua as they hugged tightly.

As Ingrid exits the washroom, Taniqua prayed. "Thank you Jesus for keeping me from sin because I was ready to, you know what, but today I can walk with integrity with my long-lost friend. Thank you. While I am thanking you Lord; could you please, please send me a faithful man. I am burning. Single life is not for me. So please hurry. I claim it and I receive it in your precious name, Amen"

Church is not so Boring

Flower Among Ash

Taniqua sat quietly in church with her children. Her eyes were cameras that captured the events of the program. Ingrid sat at the end of the same pew with her children and Ketrel.

It was the usual time when they welcome the visitors and like the other members, Taniqua glanced to see who these visitors were with not much desire to make any connection. She almost gave herself a whiplash when she quickly took a second look at one of the visitors.

Their eyes met and her draw dropped. She stared at him for the duration of the welcoming song. When she had unglued her eyes, she realized Ingrid's eyes were clued on her and him. After the welcoming song Tommy walked over to her and sat down.

"I guess it is appropriate to say hello. Finally, I am here. All those invitations you have been leaving in the lobby to get my undivided attention. I am here now: you got me", Tommy spoke to her confidently.

After the shock wore off, Taniqua replied, "It was for anyone. I did not leave the brochures there for you specifically. You are still the same old Tommy. It must be a white thing".

"You're not still into that no milk duds diet? Not in the house of the Lord where there are neither bond or free, Jews or gentile, black or white"

"I know the Bible. You do not have to quote scriptures to me", she interrupted him.

"The pastor said you should take me home for lunch" he added.

"I did not invite you here today", she corrected him.

"You did. Those brochures you place in the lobby", he

reminded her as he reached into his pocket for the expired pamphlet.

"That was like two years ago! She exclaimed.

He jokingly replied, "the address is the same".

"Whatever! Be reverent. You are in the house of God".

"And sitting beside His beautiful created being".

"You are an arrogant and clueless man Tommy", she whispered in his ear.

"You wanted to kiss me. Go ahead. God won't mind. After all He is a God of love", he breathes heavily in her ear.

"You are a sinner! She pretended to rebuke him.

"C'mon! you know you want me".

"Shhhhhhh! Be respectful in the house of the Lord" the woman in the big red hat sitting before them said intruding in their conversation. "These young people do not have any reverence for the Almighty", she informed the woman sitting next to her.

"It is the world we are living in: Godless", she replied and scoffed at them.

Tommy leaned over to address the women when Taniqua hastily pulled him back. "Enough! Now is not the time no matter how amusing you might think you are".

"Really! I amuse you or am I your muse? I will take either".

"Go home!

"What would the Lord say if I left without my blessings?

"Give it up".

"After you, my sweets".

"Shhhhh", the women interjected.

He leaned over to Taniqua, "whisper something in my ear like you did before", he suggested.

Flower Among Ash

She took the Bible and blocked his face before he got too close. She was not amused anymore. She got up in a hurry to leave her seat. She was caught up in trying to pass the other people sitting in the pew and climbing over baby bags and coloring activity books on the floor dropped by the children who are now fast asleep supported up by each other. When she had finally made it over the obstacle course and exit the pew: she looked up and there was Duquan. She lost her balance and fell on him with fright. He gripped her arm while she apologized to him. She did not want to make it obvious that she could not get out of his tight grip. She hugged him in a platonic way while patting him over his shoulder and was about to walk away thinking that was enough.

"A white man you want? He asked her in audibly for those near to hear.

She tried to get away from him but he pinned her to the wall and screamed at her. "Tell me this, you come to church to look man? What is the white boy doing here? You cannot do like I did and still be a lady. You don't hear what the song said fool"

"Let go of me! She bit his arm and the punches flew.

Tanisha was caught in the middle scramming leave my daddy alone as she too began to hit her mother.

Tommy got into it and duke it out with Duquan. The boxing match got the young people in an uproar in the sanctuary. While Taniqua stooped down in the corner trying to hide from the shame she saw her daughter in brother McLeod's hand kicking and screaming for Tommy to leave her daddy alone.

"Daddy! Daddy! She cried. "I want my dad! Put me down!

Taniqua turned her attention to Tommy and Duquan. The fight had stop. The men in the church managed to stop the fight. She did not move. In a few seconds, she heard sirens. The police came and Duquan was arrested. The scenes were turned back to her six-year-old child agonizing for the father she had not seen in weeks. She went to her grandmother for comfort.

"Are you ok? Tommy asked her.

"Please take me home", she said to him.

"No problem".

Black Blonde

Flower Among Ash

"Oh my gosh! Why did I come here? I must be losing my mind", Taniqua whispered to herself as she entered the church.

"What is it mama? Tanisha asked curiously.

"Nothing"' she replied with disbelief.

"Are you still mad at me mama? She asked with a childlike innocence.

"No! Stop bothering me and for the last time do not call me mama", she told her angrily and makes a few giant steps to walk on ahead of her daughter.

"I just want to be like you when you called your mother mama", her voice squeaked as they tried to keep up.

"Go to your Bible class and leave me alone", she replied harshly as she kept on walking.

"You hate my daddy and now you hate me".

She turned around to her daughter and looked at her angrily, "you father embarrassed me here last week and now you. Is that you want to do here in the parking lot. I am your mother and you have the nerve to fight me for your daddy. When was the last time you see him? You want to be with your daddy, next time when you see him, leave. You are an ungrateful brat!".

Taniqua was not aware that her harsh word had melted her six-year-old little heart and how she was hurting too. She had not noticed that there were a few mothers standing around shaking their heads at her parenting skill. She did not see the deaconess coming towards her until she taps her on her shoulder. She turned around like a whirlwind.

"What! She shouted her. Realizing whom it was, she apologized. "I am so sorry. I should not have come here today. I forgot about the scene her father created here last week"

"I am not here to judge you. I can relate to what you are going through. I want to encourage you and pray for you. I wanted to speak to you last week but the police came and I do not know anyone that has your number, so I am glad you came today. Come with me inside. We can find a quiet room where we can pray and talk. Come Tanisha, I want to pray for you too".

They silently walked into the prayer room with the deaconess. The pastor joined a few minutes later and spoke to them.

"I am sorry I was not able to get in touch with you earlier. I have been so busy but that is no excuse. I want to come to your home to have a prayer service with you and your children. I hope that is ok?

"Yes".

"I am very proud of you", the pastor continued.

"For disrupting the church?

"For going back to school and moving out of that situation".

"How did you know that? She asked surprisingly.

"We have been praying for you at your mother's request. I was pleased to know that God has answered your mother's prayer when she told us you went back to school. We fasted on your behalf. The prayer team has been vigilant as you are going through this and we will continue to pray for you. Before I go any further, give me your phone number and address".

As she gave the pastor the information, she said to him, "I thought I was in this alone. I know my mom wants me to do right but it is hard to be like her. Honestly, I think she hates me; at least that is how I feel most of the time. I think she is ashamed of me so this is a surprise to me that she would do all that you said. Why could she not tell me what she was doing on my behalf? I know, she is still ashamed of me though".

"I could meet with both of you to address those issues. Right now, I want to assist you, the church wants to help in any way we can. I should go now but I want you to know that we are in your corner. God is in your corner. I will keep in touch. Let's have a quick word of prayer".

After the pastor prayed the deaconess prayed for her and volunteered to take Tanisha and her brothers to their Bible class. She went to her Bible class feeling shaky, ambivalent and surprised to learned that there are people here who care about her and her children. She tried to calm herself down, trying not to stick out. She sat a distance away from the group. The teacher invited her to come closer to the group but she refused. She scanned the congregation wondering what they think of her when a girl her age came and sat next to her, almost on her lap. She was astonished.

"Hi, my name is Sandy. I've been a member here for a while but we have never met before. I am with the Pathfinder and in the choir. You should join, if you can sing or come out to support us at our concert. Have you bought your tickets yet?

Taniqua felt mummified. She was not responsive to the invasion.

"I hear you have a lot of children. How old are you? You look my age. I wanted to have a boyfriend but my parents told me not under their roof. It would kill them if after paying all that money to go to college and then get into stuff like, you know what I mean. I wish I could. Could you have a boyfriend and not get pregnant? Whenever I rebel against my parents' decision they said look at Taniqua with a truckload of children tying up her feet: they are Jamaicans, go figures. I might look like a person that does not rebel but I have feeling and needs too eh! They want me to talk to you to see how bad your life is so I will not want to do anything stupid. They did not say it in so many words, but every time I heard, look at Taniqua! Do you want to be like her! Is she your role model! As I said before, they are Jamaicans so they yell a lot. My dad took me to Jamaica for an entire summer just to whip me. Growing up, I did not like to go to Jamaica. One Easter, they tricked me and send me there by myself. Did I get it from my cousin? Can you imagine that? My cousin'"

"What is the cost of the tickets", Taniqua asked as she unfreezes.

"The prize for the tickets", she corrected her. "I will tell you that after church. You should not talk about money on the Sabbath hour".

In her comatose state, Taniqua got up and went into the hallway. Sandy joined her.

"I would love to babysit for you sometime to see how paranoid my parent is but I not trying to get pregnant or nothing like that"

Taniqua had had enough. "Have you consider tying you tubes? She asked arrogantly.

"You know what miss clueless, get out of my face. You are the first black blonde I have ever met. Oh, my gosh! I

Flower Among Ash

cannot find words to utter to you in your ignorance. Leave me alone!

"I just wanted to know where you went wrong so I can have a boyfriend and not make the same mistake like you".

"Get a clue! Taniqua yelled. You better get out of my face before I regret what I am about to do!

"I just wanted to be your friend and to help you. You should help other girls like yourself not to make the same mistake like you. You are angry all the time. My parents….

"Leave me the hell alone! Taniqua shouted at her. A flood of tears came rolling down her face. "I will never be your friend. You are not better than me. Yes, I have a truckload of children, I am always angry but you know what God still loves me". By now last week was being repeated. She had an audience circling her. "What are you looking at vultures? Every rose has thorns! As for you miss blonde, you get in my face again, you will regret it". She saw the pastor heading her way. She kept her eyes on him. He swept her away into his office. Taniqua was convinced that there was more evidence for her to leave the church than to try to go back to life she once had with Christ. Life was becoming challenging for her. The pastor excused himself after their brief talk to preach.

Taniqua was drained emotionally. She took out her cell phone from her pocket book and called for a ride. "Hi, can you do me a favor please. Pick me up now please. Church. Thanks".

What did Paul Say?

"I do not mean to bother you. You have been a big help to me. I remember the first time we met at the old place and other encounters we had back then: they were not pleasant".

"It is our fate"

"Do you really think that? I did not believe you would consider a thing like that".

"You have resisted me a long time but here we are".

"Do not get your hopes up, you are not here for the reason you think. I just want you to know that I appreciate your help, especially for getting me away from Duquan and standing up for me".

"No problem man!

"I do appreciate it a lot. Do you know in all my lifetime not one person had ever fought for me? Well, then again, all my troublesome years were with Duquan. I was so dedicated to him. I can honestly say that most of my time with him I did not think of marriage and what God think of the relationship. I just kept on popping out babies. You were right about me".

"When was I ever right? I was trying to …I was competing for your affection and I figure if I place the mirror before you to show you, you know, you would give me a chance. I do not know what came over me. You were right: I was going through my own inner conflict and wanted to fit in with people that is different than myself. I was rebelling my strict orthodox Jewish lifestyle. I want to find myself which led me to move to Parkdale.

"Can you spend the night?

"Sure"

"Not for the reason you think"

"Any reason is good enough for me. I am proud of you".

"Really?

"You left the ghetto but not the just leaving, is the way you carry yourself and the way you speak".

"I had to. I felt dumb at first. Ninety percent of the students in my classes are educated Caucasian and Chinese students. There, I am a misfit trying to find my place".

"You see! Back then you would have said white and other descriptive words", he interrupter her.

"I was not that bad. I did not like them at first especially when they look at me with scornful eyes when I speak. I was acting the fool. To be honest, I was a fool. They made me see myself as who I was and I was ashamed. My mentality was warp. They did not want to even work on projects with me. I rebel, called some of them a few unchristian-like names, and threw a fit but then I remembered what I was trying to leave behind. I called on God and the next thing my attitude changed. I humble myself, put my tail between my legs and did what I had to do".

"You people really have tails?

"I cannot believe you said that to me!

"You said that you put your tail…

"It is a figure of speech Tommy!

"I was just kidding!

"You are corny. Your sense of humor is so way off and rude".

"Now you are one of us?

"No. I had to change my image and from then my professor's attitude changed and my classmates too. I practiced reading out loud so I can sound white. I read before the mirror to see if I was making the white expression. It was frustrated. In a matter of time I was speaking using proper grammar. School does that to you. It brought me back to when I just came up from Jamaica: how I want to speak like a Canadian with the accent and all. Boy! I did fell backward. I prayed and kept going even stumbling over my tongue. That is how I got the job before I graduated. He still wants me to keep studying. He believes in me. Yesterday he told me how he marvels to see my turnaround from who I was back then. When I think about it: I was ignorant".

"Is Ketrel still you friend?

"He comes by".

"Are you in a relationship with him?

"We were always in a relationship".

"Is he still your friend?

"What is that to you?

"Something happened between you two?

"There you go again being Tommy".

"He put the moves on you, didn't he?

"Ok, I think I made a big mistake asking to stay the night".

"Did you?

"No!

"Good".

"And if I did?

"I was just thinking why you want me to sleep over and not him. I am glad he messed up. Things are working out for me."

"Tommy, the less you say, the less trouble your tongue will get you in. You are plainly not a people person. For your information, I want you to stay because Duquan is out of lock up and is querying about my whereabouts. I hope you can defend me again".

"I might be quirky but I do care. I do not believe a man should hit his woman".

"I've never seen you with a girl. I almost thought you were gay".

"Look who is not a people person. Why would you think of me in that way? It hurts me to know that such thought would enter your mind".

"I am sorry".

"And you complain about my communication skills".

"Whatever. I am going to bed. Good night".

"No goodnight kiss".

"No".

"Can I give you one?

"No".

"C'mon, throw the dog a bone".

She sighed, "I can give you a hug".

"I can live with that. You must come closer for me to hug you, for me to wrap my arms around, to hold you gingerly the way you are supposed to be held, the way….

"Stop! Or else I will change my mind. Do not say anything. Let's get it over and done with".

She was in his arms in a second. She was tense at first but he insisted he was not going to let go until she relaxes and trust that he will be with her through the night and assured her that he will not allow Duquan to hurt her. Her body relaxed at his word.

He held her face gently and said, "I am a lot of thing but this I know: I want you. I want to be with you".

Sunny Side Up

Flower Among Ash

"Good morning".

"I thought you'd left when I did not see you".

"I promised you last night that I was going to stay and beside with what happened last night I thought it would be good to make you breakfast. The children are eating. Where is Tanisha?

"She is with my mom".

"Is she still upset with you?

"We are both angry. I never thought I would be this upset at my own child. I cannot bear seeing her right now".

"You don't mean that".

"I do! She hit me at the same time her father was bashing me face in. He always goes for my face".

"So that no one else will find you attractive".

"I love her but I am still angry at her. I do not think she loves me".

"She does. Absence make the heart grow fonder. Come and have something to eat. You know what stay there, I'll bring it to you".

"Thanks. I do not feel like getting out of bed".

He brought her breakfast in bed. "Here you are my queen".

"I am nobody's queen".

"You are mine", he said with a kiss. "My queen, you are out of toilet paper and I have to go really bad".

"Thanks for spoiling the mood. Use Kleenex. Before you go; the eggs are not cooked".

"It is sunny-side up", he replied as he dashed off to use the bathroom.

Rewind and Replay

Taniqua sat with Ingrid during the youth service. Once again their children were united. It was as if they had never been apart. The service did not do much for the long parted friends as they reminisced and buried the hatchet.

"Ketrel told me he saw you down town near that college. What was it? I think it was the one you were going to".

"Yeah".

"You must have hooked up with a lot of new white friends", she continued to break the awkward silence.

"My classes are multicultural like Toronto", she answered in a tone of avoidance.

"Ketrel told me you told him that you were the only black student in most of your classes".

"I had many different classes. Some of them were all white but I was there to learn", Taniqua answered.

"I see you do not want to talk about it because what Ketrel told me. My man would not lie to me….unless..

"Ingrid, we just made up a few week ago and I do not want to spoil it".

"Catching up with my girl is not going to put a ding in our friendship. We've been friends for so long. It is not the first time we malice each other and then hook back up again", Ingrid reasoned.

"Look, when it comes to certain things you know we part company".

"Say it. When it come to your degree, you part company with me".

"Here we go again"

"But is it not true that as soon as you started to go to school we started to have problems?

"Whatever you say".

"Yep"

"Why do you have to go there? We are here having a good time and you had to go there. Just leave it alone because I am not ashamed of what I am doing. If I had not gone back to school, I would not be capable to care for my children".

"We are such good friends that you failed to tell me you are still in school. I passed all that. I wished you would share stuff with me if you want to truly remain my friend".

"You always give me mixed feelings about me going forward with my life. I would rather not talk about that part of my life with you even though we are friends. It is such an uncomfortable subject".

"If that is what you want. I feel you are still upset at me because I did not go back to school with you".

"No. I was, but not anymore. You are you and I am whom I am. I will not be satisfied with mediocre living".

"Don't preach to me: I get it!"

"Let's talk about your son's party next Saturday night!

The two were rooted in the party plans and excitement when Tanisha shouted with excitement, "Daddy! Mama, daddy is here!

Raven heard his sister and jumped across his mother. There was a loud echoing band. Raven lost his balance. Taniqua reached down to grasp him before she hit the floor. What seemed to be a few minutes were only seconds when she brought her daughter up from her near fall? She remembered hearing the echoed bang ringing in her ears, then Ingrid's scream. She looked at Ingrid with a questionable looked when at the corner of her eyes, she saw men rumbling and toppling on top of each other. In her confused state, she realized that Raven was weighing her hand down.

"Raven, get off mommy's hand", she said trying to pull her hand from under her. She did not budge. She pulled her hand out from under Raven with more force so she could attend to Ingrid who was hysterical. Her hands got loosed. Her focused were on Ingrid until she yelled and pointed at Raven.

"Taniqua! Raven! He shot Raven!

In a whiplash, she looked down on her daughter. As fast as the speed of light: she knew what had happened. Duquan was the one buried under the heap of men. She stared and waited to see his face. The deacons had him in a bind. He stared at her while she stared back without seeing him. She was blinded by the shock.

Her mother came over to her and screamed, "My grand baby. He shot his own child. What kind of mad man are you? She cried.

It was then that Taniqua understood what actually happened.

She Forgot

Flower Among Ash

"Mama, is daddy coming to Raven's funeral? He is always late. Like when he told me he was bringing the pizza and it never came. I know he is going to be late. He loves Raven. He is going to show up, right mama?

"You got to be kidding me! Who is coming to the funeral? She asked her daughter angrily.

"Daddy! Silly! What if he is going to get Raven so we do not have to bury her and we can go to the park after sunset? She paused to gather her thoughts together then spoke freely, "Mama, now I am the silly one! I forgot it is Thursday evening", she continued with a childish innocence.

"That is not all you had forgotten". She stooped down to her daughter, gripping her hands tightly, and speaking to her sternly. "I do not want to hear you talking about that man ever again", she scolded her daughter and she counted each word so that Tanisha could understand what she was saying.

"You're hurting me! Tanisha squirmed. "I want my daddy cause….

Taniqua mother saw what was going on and rushed over the separate the two. Tommy took Tanisha to the bedroom to get ready for the service while she had a talk with Taniqua.

"You must be patient with her. She is in shock about the entire incident", her mother assured her.

"She was there when her so called daddy killed her sister! My daughter mom! Taniqua broke down.

"I know but…..

"But what mom? I have been living in fear because of him. He does not support his family. She got nothing from him and she is always taking his side. She is an ungrateful little brat. I am sick and tired of this".

"Don't say that, she is just seven".

"Stop taking up for her mom! She always hated me like how you hate me. He poisons her mind against me and you know that. You keep her", she yelled at her mother.

"That is not true. I do not hate you".

"Please", she replied in disbelief.

"I know you are hurting and you have every right to lash at me but you need to ease up with Tanisha. She is a little girl. She loves her father. He was the world to her despite he was never around. I cannot explain it, only God can. Bear with her. Eventually she will come around to what happened", she said with compassion.

"Since you understand her so well, why don't you keep her? I have been through hell with that man and now I am looking over my shoulder since he escaped. You know what: if it comes to it, that little girl will give me up to him. You think she will warn me if he is coming at me to attack me?

"He is not a threat to her. You would have to; I do not know. I guess I must keep her until this pass. I do not think he will bother me. It is you he is upset with".

"Why is he upset with me? We broke up long time ago"

"What is going on with you and Tommy?

"You've been wanting to ask me that for a long time. FYI, he is just a friend".

"A friend that is sleeping at your apartment. You rededicated your life to God. You cannot engage in premarital sex with this man even if he is protecting you. Why don't you trust God to protect you? You know Duquan is jealous".

"And the other women in his life all through our relationship. He had never been faithful to me. Duquan

Flower Among Ash

does not know what it is like to be in a relationship with one woman".

"What is your excuse for having Tommy living with you?

"He is not living with me. He is just my companion temporarily. I need him there with me in the apartment just in case Duquan drops by".

"You put a man before God".

"I do not put him before anybody".

"Then what purpose is he serving there? Are you committing fornication with Tommy? That displeases God and you….

"Get off my case mother: I am through trying to please you".

"It is not about me. You were doing so well for months being active in the church and continuing with your study. Do not turn from the right path Taniqua".

"He is good to me and besides he is there just in case Duquan shows up".

"God can do better: let him".

"Do not judge me. I have no time for this. Now is not the time to be standing over me with the Ten Commandments. So, I fell off the gospel wagon! Sue me".

"Do not make things get worse by getting into anything with Tommy. He is a nice guy and all but there are other ways to do this".

"Do what mom? He is more of a man to me that Duquan had ever been to me"

"You do not have to sleep with him for that Taniqua".

"I cannot talk to you about this now or ever because you are always looking down at me hoping for me to fail. Maybe religion is not for me".

"Don't tell me you are pregnant again".

"That is just what I am talking about. That look of disappointment. It is just like me to fail you. Say it. I am a failure"

"Is he going to marry you?

"I thought Duquan would marry me and he did not. I am not the marrying type and besides, he does not know that I am pregnant".

"He knows now", Tommy interjected.

The Testimony

Flower Among Ash

After a day of prayer and fasting, Taniqua walked up to the mic to share her testimony. Tommy and Taniqua had eloped before her stomach start showing. Her conscience was troubled and she decided to give a testimony.

"Good evening saints. I first want to thank the church for being there for me during the loss of my daughter and the encouragement I got in dealing with Tanisha. I know many of you know me as the girl who have been living contrary to the church beliefs. I have been through a lot and have done many things that I've regretted. This morning I got baptized; again, for the third time hoping to please God and my mother. I lost myself and forgot what I wanted. I found Jesus in all my mistakes and I am asking you to pray for me that this time I will walk on the straight and narrow. I was living in fear of my ex and rely on a man for protection when I should have depended on God. You cannot see it but I am expecting. Knowing my mom: some of you might have already know about it. It is not like I am not trying to live right but things got in the way. Thanks to the power of your prayers, when Duquan came to apartment while Tommy was there and the children that everything ended well. I am probably not making sense to you but I am sincerely grateful for your support". She paused and took a deep breath of courage. "I want you to continue to pray for me now that I am going to have Tommy's child and mom I am sorry. Tommy and I eloped yesterday. I am his wife. If you had told me in the past that I would marry a Caucasian man, I would not have believed you. I was illiterate and dumb back then. He is my husband and he treats my very well. Please pray for us. I can truly say I am happy. I am doing well in school, getting good grades and most times, I am top in my classes. Me, the high school drop-out. The teen mom. The trouble kid. In Jamaica, they have this saying ***finger stink, do not cut it off.*** I could feel my mother breathing down on my neck and I hated it. It annoyed me as I tried to get it together. I am glad that my mother set the stage for me to follow in this Christian walk. I have fallen many times with scares to last me a lifetime but here I am: I am on my feet again with God and a good man. Thank you for your prayers. I want to thank the church for not giving up on me. I mostly thank God for not giving up on me".

Later that day Taniqua went over to her mother's house. She opened the door with her spare key. Her mother was sitting in the living room and spoke immediately as they entered the house.

"Why could you not say anything to me about it? The mother is the last to know"

"Good evening to you too mom. I am not going to start a fight with you today. I thought you would be happy with me now that I am married and re-baptized. What must I do to please you?

"I had to know about your marriage in front of the entire church"

"You were not in front of the entire church".

"You know what I meant".

"This is all about us and me making it right with God. Is not that what you want?

"I wanted you to let God fix the problem. You are always trying to do God's work".

"Be happy for me. If you are not happy for me, it will be your choice but this is it. I though you like Tommy".

"Do you think what you did and how you announced your nuptial is going to make things better?

Tommy broke his silence and spoke up, "I think I've heard enough. This is my wife. I am not concern about her past. I am more interested in where we are going. I thought we were getting along fine. I am not sure about how you feel about me now and I am sorry that you were not there at our wedding but having a baby is a big deal to me and I was not going to wait to make her my wife. I am nothing like Duquan. I have done my share of mistakes but I will not let my child enters the world out of wedlock and besides, I love your daughter before things had gotten this badly. I am a man of my words. I will be faithful to one wife and one wife only. I understand that this is a shocker but what is done, is done and if I had the chance to do it all over again, I still would want to marry Taniqua. She is the woman for me regardless of the internal spiritual conflict she is going through. I can relate. So please, I do want your support. If you choose not to support us, please do not upset her and it is not just for the baby. I believe Taniqua has had her full share of hurt and disappointment".

"I am not accusing you to be anything like Duquan but.

"That is my mother Tommy, there is always a but" Let's go home. You've proved to me that it has not always been all that I did that put a riff in our relationship. I cannot meet your expectation. You are so accustomed to see me fail that even when I got it right, you are still waiting for me to fail. Come Tommy, let's go home and mother, can't you see that I have risen from the ash?

CPSIA information can be obtained
at www.ICGtesting.com
Printed in the USA
BVOW03s2358060817
491331BV00001B/1/P